NEVER SQUEEZE

a

HONEYBEE!

THE CONTINUING ADVENTURES
OF NATHANIEL B. OAKES

NATHANIEL B. OAKES

Published by J.D. Oakes Publishing, LLC
Spokane, WA
www.jdoakes.com

ISBN: 978-0-9844832-6-6

Printed in the United States of America

CONTENTS

To Mom and Dad,
Whose bountiful love nourished this sprightly brood,
And to my brothers and sisters
who sprouted so wondrously there from.

And especially many heart felt thanks
to my wife, Clarabelle,
who tends and mends me and the children.

.

My wife Clarabelle and I, with all the six children, spill out of a roomier car than my pickup and into the yard of my childhood home. Only this time, it's not the song of the crickets that meets me; no, it's early spring and the symphony of frogs' love songs are what fill the late evening air. The songs waft in cadences that range from booming bass to lilting contralto. Crickets in the late fall, frogs in the early spring. There are myriads of frogs that inhabit the ponds in the old mine behind our place. Yes, this time it's the singing frogs that start turning the pages in my memory of the delightful days spent in my childhood on the farm. Listen! Closely...and turn the pages to once again run in the playground of my youth.

Oh! Ah yes! And how did my wife get that endearing delightful name, Clarabelle? Well, she requested it. You see, as a child my family had June, Pixie, Pumpkin, Millie, and Polly as family cows; and now I own Annabelle and Mishki. Oh yeah, there's Sue Ellen, the milk cow across the fence. I even hear there might be a Bobbie Sue joining us, too. That's a lot of bovine beauty to be surrounded with and with all the attention it requires to maintain these cows, my wife was just feeling downright left out. So she changed her name to Clarabelle, and now she fits right in with the rest of the characters on the farm, where she can get the attention she deserves.

BIKER'S LAMENT

"All you have to do is put your foot down if you are going to fall over," said Marisa patiently. I had attempted this before many times, but as I began to fall over Marisa would have to catch me and put me upright again. This is how I faced the perils of riding a bike for the first time. I found it difficult to get the courage to let loose of the secure pedal with my foot.

You see, Marisa was teaching me to ride a bike. She was finding it a bit difficult to get my pointy elbows, knobby knees, skinny fanny, and all the various ligaments that hold it all together, to balance this two-wheeled contraption. Life was not going to be easy, I began to intuit. Too many times I had heard the expression when some reluctant person was being cajoled into a doubtful activity, "Oh, it's no problem. It's as easy as riding a bike." If this was easy, life was going to be hard.

We stood this time at a place way up the driveway, about 50 yards away from the house, what we referred to as the 'end of the property.' The end of the 40 acres stopped here and the 30-foot wide easement of dirt road leading out to the county road continued from there.

I again eased my 6-year-old body onto a little, faded, old blue bike. It wasn't a big kid's bike, but it wasn't a little kid's bike, either. It was sort of an in-be-tweener. Marisa held firmly on the back of the seat as I clambered onto the bike and got my feet firmly placed on the pedals.

Thus, perched precariously with my posterior on the wide broad metal seat, my feet dangling a frightening 4 inches above the ground, I was ready to go. Meanwhile, Dad, unbeknownst to us, was getting ready to mow the front lawn. Now the lawn was bordered by round poles lying on the ground. They were about 12 feet long and 4 inches in diameter. Dad had moved these out of his way by rolling them onto the driveway, so that he wouldn't have to trim around them.

Marisa was unaware of these new obstacles in our path, so she concentrated on telling me just what to do if I lost balance. "This time as I run behind you holding onto the seat, just start pedaling and when you are going well, I'll let go. I'll run behind you in case you fall. Just remember to turn towards where you think you are going to fall and put your foot down." This advice coming from Marisa should have been taken a little warily. She's the one who couldn't always get her feet to agree with one another and upending her without notice.

I nodded that I was ready and we were off. Marisa pushed and I pedaled. We picked up speed. Dad meanwhile picked up another log and placed it on the driveway. I pedaled more confidently. A breeze began to tease my hair. I sailed faster. Another log placed on the driveway by Dad. Marisa let go. She yelled. "Remember to put your foot down." I gained more speed. Marisa couldn't keep up. I began to list to the left. A fleet panic tried to catch me for a moment, but I steered into the list and I was again upright. For a moment, I was an iconic Norman Rockwell 'boy on bike,' cruising blissfully along. I rolled along unaware of the one last log Dad was rolling onto the driveway. I was quickly approaching the front lawn now and I began to lose my balance. I began to lean to the right, so I corrected to the right. It didn't work. I began to fall to the right. 'Put your foot down, put your foot down!" screamed Marisa.

And I did. Right onto a log that Dad had just rolled onto the driveway and which I now paralleled. My foot hit the log. The logged rolled. I went crashing down. My chin hit the steel nut that holds the handlebars to the yoke. For a split second I thought my jaw had the better part. It wasn't so. My chin was split. Blood gushed. I hollered. Dad rushed over. Marisa felt awful, and Mom had to take me to the doctor. I got one whole stitch.

Now a stitch is a pretty important thing. It meant a chocolate bar on the way home to try to mollify my traumatic experience. It meant celebrity treatment when I got home, as all the other kids gathered about to see my stitch; and if it left a respectable enough scar, it would look like I got in a fight with a pirate. Well, of course I won; I am here, aren't I? And the pirate is nowhere to be found.

But one stitch only goes so far. So with a different bike when I was a bit older, I tried to increase the number of stitches. I wanted to get a ride in before dinner.

I was up what we called the mind road. Mind road? Yes, mind road. To the older siblings it was probably a mine road, but to us youngsters it was the mind road. It was the white gravel road that paralleled our dirt driveway for about an eighth of a mile, until it turned sharply up the hill into the old silica mine. The old mine bordered the west property line of our farm. That road went up a fairly steep incline for a couple of hundred yards, meandered to the left still farther up and divided into many smaller roads, which led to all sorts of neat places to entice small boys into adventure.

This time, I was gripping the handlebars of an old red bike. In most particulars it was a good bike. Jeremy had used it for awhile and then he handed it down to me. Well, not all of it down to me. Most of it down, I'd say. One essential thing was missing: the chain. Now, bike chains and we boys never could quite see eye-to-eye as to just what they were made for. The chain thought eating pant legs when you were bar-reling down the road with a mean dog after you was a critical start to a proper chain's life. If not that, to break and leave the bike and fly into the bushes when a good swift brake was needed. Or to eat your finger as you tried to coax it back onto a sprocket when you were on the fly.

Just staying on the sprockets and propelling the bike forward to get a boy from point A to point B, with no harm to the boy or the bike, just wasn't excit-ing enough for the chains on our bikes. They seemed always to be breaking or causing trouble. It was a constant battle that we boys fought with these stub-born or wayward bike chains. Sometimes we would buy a new link to replace an old one that broke, but this cost money, so often baling wire and old nails had to be commandeered into service to do the job. This would get us up and running, but these makeshift repairs were not real trustworthy and often left us in the lurch.

And a lurch is what I was now in. The chain on this bike that Jeremy had handed down to me had broken on Jeremy. It had flown into the bushes as he raced down the road a while before, and it needed repair once again. Well, this time the thought of finding and bending an old nail to put back together the old chain was too much. So I just pushed this bike up the mine road, determined to get a good, fast coast in before dinner anyhow.

When I reached a good ways up, I lined myself up with an old concrete dynamite shed that was left over from the mining days, and surveyed the road below. I could just see the sharp turn I would have to make when the road ceased to be perpendicular to our driveway and began to run parallel to it. This should be a fun coast. So I shoved off.

I placed my feet firmly on the pedals and let gravity do its work. It pulled me down the hill. The road began to travel a little faster under my feet as I got under way. My exhilaration picked up along with the speed. Exhilaration and speed became friends, cheering each other on to make even greater swiftness. I swelled with joy, but just to make sure I instinctively applied backward pressure on the pedals to make certain the friendly brakes would be there when needed, if speed and exhilaration tried to lead me to a perilous end. Uh, oh! There was no pressure. With a little alarm I back- pedaled a little more expecting the chain to catch. It didn't. Wait! There was no chain! I had forgotten, so I tried to rejoin in the friendship of speed and exhilaration, but in their excitement they had forgotten about me. Exhilaration was leaving me for the more exciting speed. It left me clutching the handlebars firmly with rising apprehension. It was fine for a couple of adjectives to try to make the turn that was quickly approaching. If they wrecked and their parts got splattered about, they could easily be put back together again and perhaps changed, with only a couple letters mangled and changed around, to rest and relaxation and nobody gets hurt. I was made of more substantial matter and risked life and limb. Life was about the only thing my limbs possessed, a little muscle only came later, so life was critical to my limbs and I was determined to keep them together.

Now sometimes the danger one anticipates is not the one that transpires. As my eyes began to bulge in anticipation of running into the trees and bushes if I failed to make the rapidly approaching turn I grasped the handlebars more tightly to make sure I still had control with me. My tires bit into a sea of loose gravel. Not ordinary gravel, but ornery vicious gravel. Chewed up silica gravel! It's pretty, but deceptive. Chewed up silicon crystals make for very sharp rocks and this whole road had been graveled with these mine tailings. This is the trap that my tires plunged into. Caught in this, speed and exhilaration tried to continue with their wild ride but were upended. As my tires bit into this deep soft trap I began to weave. First to the left it pulled. I strained to yank the handlebars to the right. The slushy gravel dragged on my tires and my front tire hove to the left and then the right as I wrestled with the handlebars to keep control. The vicious gravel's pointy fingers clutched at my tires. Control sailed over the handlebars with speed and exhilaration.

I tried not to follow them but couldn't resist. Those three fickle friends left me and my bike, control leading. The front tire was stuck firmly in the silica claws. Momentum carried the rear tire up and the seat launched me into the air to sail after my friends. This could not be good. I had to land. So I did. My right knee hit first, my other extremities hit next in no particular order. The silica gravel bit deeply into my knee and from there I tumbled and skidded upon the sharp silica gravel. I came to a sliding stop. I shakily sat up and shook the cobwebs out of my head. Whew! The gravel extracted, I wouldn't say a pound of flesh, but it scraped what it could, leaving me with a very respectable gash on my right knee, my elbows gave up skin and a shoulder bone was a bit sharpened.

So I raised myself a bit wobbly off the ground and picked up my bike to assay the damage to it. The handlebars were wrenched to the side, but that was all it had suffered. Next, I stretched around to get my ligaments and limbs to line up. I found I could still walk, so I started the long push home. Blood ran freely down my mangled knee and drenched my sock.

Mom patched me up when I got home. I danced and whined as she washed the cut with soap and water. The question now was. Would Davy Crockett go get stitches for this? Leo offered to find a cat and sew it up with catgut stitches. Sounded neat to me, real frontier like, although the thought of a wooden needle and catgut with Leo poking into my knee did give me pause. Mom told Leo that that was not helpful and bound up my wound with abundant white doctor's tape and white gauze. It wasn't bad. I'd seen pictures of Civil War soldiers bound up like this. So I didn't get stitches, and my cut turned into a good scar. Pretty Davy Crockett like, don't you think?

Pretty well-healed up from that chainless bike adventure, I was positioned to try another. The turn I was apprehensive to take is described in the last episode. It banked so as to make it more navigable for the mine trucks, as they came down out of the mine. This left the downside of the bank to spill down and meet our driveway. It had become all overgrown with bushes and a few pine trees. We called this little knob and embankment the 'little hill.' It was about an eighth of a mile up the driveway. The driveway continued another eighth of a mile up to the county road where our mail boxes were placed. So, as you traveled up the driveway from the house, you passed the end of the property, than the little hill and then to the mailboxes, a quarter of a mile total. I was parked at the little hill. I had left Tristan playing down by the old 36′ flatbed, which was very near the loop at the house end of the driveway. I told him to watch as I rooster tailed around it. Experience had tried to teach me a little about chainless bikes. It was too little. So here I was once again positioned to make a good coast. This time I faced down the driveway; we always called it road, as in "can we go play up the road," or "can we go up the road?" So from henceforth, I will call it the road.

The driveway or road went past the house a little ways and ended in a loop, so when driving down one just went down around the loop and again faced up the driveway ready to go again. In the summer, this dirt on the loop became pulverized into soft powder from the many turns the car made on it. It was great fun to ride our bikes down the road and then make this turn as fast as we could without spilling; watching the rooster tail of dust leave a cloud behind us as the tires pounded the turf and as they tried to keep traction as we sped around it. An electric fence ran tangentially by the loop and sort of hemmed it in, so to wander from the track when going around the loop was perilous. Hitting it could lead to a nasty shock and we always gauged our speed accordingly so as not to hit the electric fence.

It was the challenge of this loop that led me to push off now from my station at the hill and begin my coast down. The start was slow at first. Respectable after a couple of minutes, it got definitely better as I coasted faster, then it got really good. Wow was I really moving!

As I gained more speed, I increasingly became puffed up with exuberance. I stretched my head up and back and let the cool evening air fill my lungs and spill up and over my head and whip past my ears. Unfortunately, Norman Rockwell was not around to capture this rural scene. He should have been. He might have become famous.

Soon I was nearing even with the house, and a glimmer of apprehension gripped me. I was really moving in earnest now. Could I really make the loop? I lowered my head a mite and began to assay the fast-approaching situation. Apprehension gripped a little tighter. I began the habitual ritual of applying the brakes when speed is racing you towards danger. It's then when reality fully dawned on me. Apprehension turned into real fear. There was no chain! It took no complicated calculation to figure that impending disaster was imminent. I was going way too fast. Panic made me attempt what I knew was impossible. I pedaled backwards as fast as I could in a desperate attempt to slow myself down. Tristan glanced up from where I had left him playing by the old truck and watched. He was bewildered at this new phenomenon he thought I had invented. *Neat* he thought *how the faster Nathanial pedaled backwards the faster forward Nathanial flew.* Ridiculous or brilliant he was interested and stood up to watch the show. I was too engrossed in my predicament to appreciate Tristan's philosophical musings. I stopped pedaling and braced myself as I entered the turn. As I leaned into the turn, powdered dirt flew in beautiful rooster tails from my tires, but my eyes were glued to the road and my jaws were clenched in desperate concentration. I had no time to look at them as I rounded the turn.

At this speed I had to lean my bike even further to turn sharper. I leaned so far over that my eyes caught the surprised look of a grasshopper sunning himself on the dirt. Simultaneously, I blinked, he winked and my tires let go. I was almost halfway around the turn and the electric fence was just feet away and I didn't want to go down. My knee and a good gash were already well acquainted and I just had to let that relationship go. So with incredible biker's skill and a tiny bit of luck I righted the bike, only to stare goggle-eyed at the impending electric fence, for as I righted the bike it also stopped me from turning and now up straight I shot at the fence. Pictures danced in my head of cows running gleefully out of the pasture, of Dad's consternation that the fence was down, and the anticipated ride into the rough field. It left me trans-fixed and glued to my bike.

For a fleeting moment I was an onlooker at a slow-motion picture show. One of those frames showed a very nice picture of a boy's bike, — not a girl's bike! Definitely it was a genuine boy's bike. It had a beauti-ful steel pipe frame running from the yoke that held the handlebars on, back to just under the seat. That frame froze the image of that pipe into my imagina-tion so that when imagination turned into reality, there could be no mistake. I knew I was in for it.

The yoke of the bike hit the wire fence and snapped it in two. I was shot into the pasture where gopher mounds and holes pogged by cow's feet abounded. Mayhem broke loose. My bike leaped and bucked. When the bike hit a really big mound my fanny raised high into the air, my feet flew off the pedals. My hands were clutched in a death grip on the handlebars. I missed the seat on the way down. I landed squarely on the bike frame (Remember that boy's bike pipe?) with my feet flailing wildly out of control. The bike continued to leap and buck. Each time I came down to meet the frame one more descendant was erased from the family tree. It seemed as if manhood would be only a sweet dream and I would be riding a girl's bike for the rest of my forlorn years.

Of the 37 seven species of bug, bird and beast that watched this ludicrous action, 17 laughed themselves silly and 20 cried in commiseration. It was a pitiable sight. The bike began to tire after a few generations of my descendants were lost. My feet finally found the ground. I dug my heels into the turf and brought that bouncing beast to a stop. I very gingerly raised my right leg over the bike frame and wheeled out of the pasture towards the house. Doubled over and barely able to walk I pushed past the beehives, which stood next to the big apple tree in the back yard. I looked plaintively over to them and begged one to come and sting me. What a pleasure to the agonies I bore. No nurse bee volunteered. They were sure enough ready to administer a sting when Dad and I went for their honey. Where were they now when I needed them? I slumped my shoulders over the bike a little more and bore my agonies to the back porch. There I crumbled into a heap. Tristan came over and sat quietly beside me. He could see that something had gone terribly wrong.

Wait and cry with me a little. Just a little... Well, maybe a little longer. Okay, I'm fine. Hurry! Turn the page or you'll miss the next adventure.

FIRE!

"The house is on fire"! Tristan yelled from the top of the plateau. For a split second the rest of us boys froze in shocked silence. We stared wide-eyed at Tristan who looked down at us, his eyes even bigger with dread.

Tristan, Damien, and I were trying to scale an

almost impossible side hill with our bicycles. We were up in the old silica mine behind our house. Mine tailings had been dumped or pushed about by the miners, which left huge rolling humps of rocky dirt. These were now overgrown with weeds and brush and a few saplings. When the old miners left, there remained 40 acres of hills, valleys, crevices, ponds and cliffs. Adventures lurked furtively all through these, and we were in the process of un-lurking one.

The bikes we were trying to scale the side hill with were huge machines. These bikes' wheels were almost 4 feet in diameter, with big balloon tires and handlebars as large as Texas longhorns' horns. The seats were as round as Paul Bunyan's dinner plates. There was, consequently, a unique technique to get one of these behemoths going. First, you had to shove off the ground while pushing hard against the handlebars. Then you had to stand on the pedals and grip the handlebars firmly as you pushed down on the pedals with all your might. If you got a little speed and didn't fall over, you were off. Your head would bob up and down, and your behind would sway from side to side as you would stand first on one pedal and then the other. With momentum pitching in to help, you could really get moving. But then you had to lurch yourself up onto the seat and continue vigorously pedaling from there. Stopping the beast was an altogether different story.

This adventure was being played out on the southern end of the old mine on what we called Weedy Hill. Mom and Dad had left for town and had left 15 cents on the kitchen table in case we needed to make a phone call. This seldom happened as we didn't have a phone and to make the call required a three mile ride in a car or on a bike. A phone booth stood forlornly along the highway a few miles from our home, hoping for a chitchat to enliven its loneliness. We gladdened its existence occasionally by placing a call. The toll was 15 cents. Having deposited this on the table, they said their goodbyes and we were left to adventuring.

Now Weedy Hill's shape had a stepped contour, which faced us. It started out from the bottom as a steep 25-foot incline, and then leveled onto a small flat, and then continued up the hill. It was this small flat that we were trying to reach by scaling this 25-foot incline with our bikes.

The surrounding mine tailings and bushes allowed us room for about a 50-foot long run at it. Before starting out, we had to place our bike's rear tire close to the edge of a gully behind us. If we backed any farther, we would pitch backwards over the side and tumble into the bushes below. Thus, perilously placed, we could just eke out this 50-foot run. This gave us a fighting chance to get up enough speed before reaching the bank and then flying up in an attempt to master the top.

I was poised at the edge of the crevice for just a moment and then shoved off to make another run at the bank after my last failed attempt. I launched myself pell-mell at the hill in the ungainly manner of bopping and weaving, past described in goading these bike beasts to go. I hurtled myself towards the hill with gusto; hit the first ascent with momentum firmly behind me. I shot up the face of the hill and my eyes locked on the top edge of the bank. I continued pedaling furiously, but my speed quickly drained away. Straining every nerve and muscle, I tried to force the pedals down to drive myself up. Traitorous momentum gave up the fight and left me to my own devices.

Tristan leaned over the edge with outstretched hands to try and catch me if I could not quite make it. I was so close. All of my speed left and I stopped momentarily 3 feet from the top; my bike was vertical and there was nowhere to go but back down backwards! My eyes fastened on the edge of the bank and I held on. The bike's tires gripped the top edge of the bank with tenacity as I strained to go up, but my eyes began to pull from their sockets. Tristan swung wildly trying to grab me and almost tumbled over the edge in an effort to save me.

My eyes lost their grip and sprang back into their sockets so hard I could see what was to come behind me. I plunged back down the hill backwards from which I had so eagerly come up frontwards. My feet were off the pedals, desperately trying to grip the gravel and weeds. My toes tried to punch through the soles of my shoes to grasp the turf. But these soles were not ephemeral souls of which matter could pass through easily. No. These were genuine vulcanized man-made material soles and they were not to be punctured from inside or out. These particular soles had been trod upon so often that there was no more tread; and they did what tread less soles do, they slipped and they slid and were no match for momentum that thought it was great fun to switch sides and now pushed me down from the top. So as I gained momentum backwards, one sole lost its grip entirely and I rolled to the side and slid, and then tumbled with my bike to the bottom.

Battered, bruised and bleeding, I picked myself up, inspected my bike and headed back for the gully. I inched my rear tire to its edge in order to try again. This was fun! Tristan yelled encouragement from the top and Damien from the bottom. Give it another go! But it was just then that our attention was arrested by something much more urgent.

"Fire!" Tristan shrieked, looking wide-eyed at me from his perch on the hill. It took a moment for the word to soak in to my mind. When the full realization hit me I yelled, "Let's go!" Tristan whirled, jumped on his bike and flew off the hill like a hawk after prey. Damien leapt to his pedals. All three of us started for home with wild abandon. Adrenalin kicked in and joined abandon and we were in for a ride. It was a crazily erratic downhill ride. We pedaled frantically through weeds, brush and boulders. Sticks, stones and sand blipped by as our bikes leapt and bucked in their mad dash down the hill. We zigged and we zagged, got slapped and whacked, trying to get to the house as quickly as possible. Battered but not beleaguered, we burst onto a big plain of huge cobblestones. When we hit our bikes' big balloon tires bounced so hard over the uneven surfaces that our handlebars were like jackhammers pounding up and down. Our arms were like wet spaghetti noodles vibrating rapidly. Our jaws chattered uncontrollably as our teeth were practically jarred right out. Fighting and struggling for control, we pedaled furiously towards home.

The cobblestone field ended at a brink. With no time to think much less brake we flew over its edge. Me first, yelling "Watch it!" and Tristan and Damien following with whoops and whaaas, escaping from their wide open mouths. We clung desperately to the longhorn handlebars as our fannies left their seats and our feet rose into the air. There we flapped in the wind as our bikes descended to meet the ground. They met. Our fannies dropped and met the seats. The seats had huge springs in them. Our fannies again left their seats and we were launched into the air again. The bikes bounced once more on their balloon tires and settled on the ground. We crashed down onto our bikes and this time stayed put. Adrenalin and momentum had stayed with us through this peril and we again peddled furiously.

I yelled to Damien. "You call the fire trucks." He shouted back. "I don't have 15 cents!" I hollered to Tristan. "You get the hose and hook it to the faucet!" We were nearing the end of our ride now. Judging it was faster to leave the bikes and run through the woods the rest of the way to the house, we jettisoned the bikes. Hollywood stars would have blushed at the amateurish ways they dismounted horses on the run if they would have seen us dismount our speeding bikes on the fly. We jumped off our pedals and flew in a high arc over the boy's bike bar and hit the ground running; the loosed handlebars letting the bikes stray where they might. We tore through the woods towards home. I caught a glimpse of the bedroom window glowing in the dusk. Visions of flames leaping from the roof and then telling Mom and Dad that the house burned down all crowded my fevered imagination. I raced closer. All was quiet. The window glowed and my heart sank. The glow of the fire in the window shriveled my soul.

As I burst out of the woods I once again yelled to Tristan to grab the hose and to Damien to call the fire department. Damien said again. "But I don't have 15 cents!" Not having time to heed what he was saying, I sped through the front yard, rounded the side of the house, and shot down the north side of the house. I tried to make the last turn around the next corner to the back door with such speed that I was surely to slip and crash. Since my soul had shriveled at the sight of the glowing window, it had shrunk slightly and was loosened to fall down to the bottom of my feet where it met the soles of my shoes. Yes, those poor worn-out cousins had no tread left to tread with. At another time these two might have passed pleasantries, but not now. My soul pleaded with Sole to find traction, and fast. That lowly sole was raised to saintliness that day. It didn't find traction, it did better. It found grip. So now that the soles of my shoes had united with grip, they gripped; they didn't slip, and my soul swelled with new found hope and filled my body with strength. I exploded through the back door, nearly crashed into the stove, and pulled up short, only to find Peter doing the dishes at the sink with the most serene air of non-chalance that a life of unruffled calm could conjure. "Where's the fire?" I gasped in unbelief. He looked at me a little surprised at my ungraceful entrance into the house.

"What fire?

My body began to loosen and sag as all the pent-up energy ebbed away. I turned and walked weakly out of the house to find Tristan desperately trying to get the hose hooked to the faucet and Damien saying plaintively once more. "I don't have 15 cents." I quickly said there was no fire, and we all stood there for a moment, a little stunned. Then relief flooded over us and we regained our composure. "I didn't have 15 cents," Damien said again half plaintively.

What was this about? Not having 15 cents. Oh, now we got it. Now we got it. You see, we didn't have a phone at the time as I said before. Three miles away, up along the highway there stood a stand-alone phone booth. This is where we would drive to make a phone call, if necessary. We laughed. We laughed harder when it dawned on us that this habit was so ingrained in Damien that the phone to use was up along the highway and that he would need 15 cents for the toll that he didn't think of any other. We could imagine him toiling three miles up to the highway with his 15 cents when he could just ride to a neighboring farmer a quarter of a mile away and use their phone.

And did Peter yell fire? No. All we could figure is that some farmers who were collecting hay from the field across the 40 acres were cajoling each or some such, and as the sound wafted its long way to Tristan in the distance, it sounded like fire. We never did know. But we knew this. It was sure nice to see a glow in the window that spoke of coziness and home than something more infernal.

TIRES

The mine property that bordered our western property line was about 40 acres in size. The interior of this parcel consisted of mine tailings. These were piled in no particular order and all the hills and valleys, crevices and cliffs had their own character. My older siblings remember the last of the quality silica as it was mined out. There were remnants of the quality silica strewn about. These crystals were nearly as clear as glass and we would find many fascinating chunks as we explored and played in this abandoned landscape. A few of the old rock crushers were dynamited, much to the fright and delight of Leo and Andy, and then left deserted. We would play in these also. These rock crushers had been made out of cement and even when blown apart, huge chunks remained, which had rooms still intact.

I remember well the miners and their trucks as they hauled the inferior rocks into town for a few years after the quality ones were exhausted. Eventually even this stopped and the mine was abandoned. The miners had left a band of trees surrounding the whole mine. It varied in width as it wound itself around the mine's 40 acres, sort of a buffer between it and the surrounding farm land. It was about a 50-yard wide swath of trees as it bordered the west side of our property.

In the back southwest quadrant of the mine, there proudly stood the last remnant of a silica mountain that had arisen from the landscape around. At the very base of it in the back, where the miners left it virtually untouched, there was trees and a wood that still housed deer and other critters. As one rose higher up the remnant of the mountain the trees melted away until at the top was baldness. The rounded top was about 20 feet in diameter. Now that described the back side of the remnant. The front of it was a cliff, a white sheer cliff, which rose 200 feet from ground.

This cliff looked over what we called the Pit. The Pit was about a 200-yard in diameter crater.

The side of the crater looking towards our house had been gouged out, so that the big lagoon that had begun to form could drain out. Before this cut was made, I remember as a very small boy having hiked down into this crater with Leo, Andy, Jake and Jeremy. After toiling halfway up the inside of the crater on our way back I remember turning and looking back down to the bottom again. There etched vividly in my imagination were three ponds: a clear one, a green one, and a red one. Different minerals accounted for the different colors. It was beautiful. But unfortunately, the rain and springs filled the crater and turned it into a big lake. The miners must have thought this unsafe and blasted a hole into the side of the crater and this gouge drained the lake. After that a few small ponds would form in the bottom of the Pit. These ponds held lots of frogs.

This sheared off hill that formed the cliff we called the Peak. A misstep at the top would have ended our short life. After all the hours we spent throwing rocks off the cliff, shooting our slingshots at passing birds and being upended by our brothers as they pretended to throw us off, it's a wonder one of us hadn't sailed off it ourselves.

Now what does all this have to do with tires? Well, it doesn't really have to do with tires. No, I'm not talking just any tire, but *The Tire*. We got a lot of mileage out of playing with old car tires. Dad had gotten about 30 of them from a guy at work. These he used for holding down tarps, which protected the haystacks. When relieved of that duty these tires became our toys. We each had our favorite ones to roll. Jeremy had the neatest one. His was an old slick from a speed roadster. We would push these tires up the hills in the mine and let go from the top to see whose could go the farthest. Jeremy's would almost always win. The sidewalls on his met the tread surface at almost a right angle instead of the more rounded street tires we had. These sharp edges kept his going in a nice straight line regardless of what obstructed it; it mowed through or over things, whereas our tires tended to veer off course a lot more easily.

Now we had tried many times to roll our tires all of the way down the side hill of the Peak that faced our property. It was difficult to walk from the top of the peak down this side. It began very steep, and continued steep for about 200 yards and then began to level off a little more; it finally became flat at the woods that bordered our fence.

Now this was no cakewalk from the top to the bottom. As a matter of fact, in all those years I never saw a cake even try it. That fact alone lends veracity to my claim. No, it started bare at the top, then turned weedy as you descended and then brushy and then small saplings. Boulders strewn around and throughout, plateaus, small cliffs, crevices, bare dirt patches and the like greeted one on your descent. Running from the top of the cliff home required some guts, though we sometimes did. You were likely to be strewn amongst or splattered upon the boulders, when leaping, lurching and leaning landed you lop-sided. If you didn't lean, lurch, swerve and curve through weeds, rocks and limbs, you would upend with your end up. Flailing and floundering at speeds slightly faster than our legs could keep up, we would run down the steep hill, racing to the house and hollering to each other that the last one there was a rotten egg.

Now the car tires we had just couldn't coast all the way down this hill through so many obstacles, no matter how hard we tried. One day as we played Cowboys and Indians we discovered, somewhat buried and overgrown with weeds, *The Tire*. Yes, this tire demanded respect. It was big, scarred, and worn, but we could see it could roll. It was a tire off one of the mine trucks. These were the big over-the-road semi-trucks and their tires were huge. We could see that this tire had many years of experience rolling and it just might be able to get done what we never dreamed possible, which was to get a tire to roll all the way down this hill and beyond into the woods.

First we dug this behemoth out of the dirt and weeds. When we finally got it out, it took us all considerable effort to stand it up. We did, though. Jake, Jeremy and I began to push it up towards the peak. One of us boys was pushing straight from behind, the other two from a little to the side to keep it from falling over. Sweat poured from our brows and into our eyes as we strained to move it uphill. Sometimes even our best efforts were not enough and it would fall over and almost squash us. We felt like Sisyphus and his boulder. We had one advantage over him, though. We weren't condemned to never getting it to the top, although it seemed just as unlikely under ordinary circumstances. Three boys who together probably didn't weigh as much as this tire looked overmatched. It's just that what we lacked in bulk we made up with determination; we pressed all the determination at our disposal into service. The tire inched its way up the hill. We had a few Sisyphusion mishaps, though. As we pushed and strained it would sometimes get off kilter; we would lose our grasp and the tire would attempt to take off down the hill. With Jeremy crying "Watch it!" I'm shouting "Stop it!" Jake would lunge into a flying tackle and knock it over before it could pick up speed. Sometimes it would take all three of us to pounce on top of it to stop its downward escape, and we would sit exhausted on top of it to catch our breath as it rested on its side.

All this effort paid off one time and finally we sat triumphantly on top of the Peak, on the tire. We congratulated ourselves as we surveyed the panorama that spread before us. It was a beautiful sight. Our eyes gathered in Mount Spokane in the far eastern distance, then rode undulating farmland that broke out from the trees, which skirted the mine all around. They next climbed up hills and the mountains, which circled away off in the distance and finally came to rest there in enchantment.

This reverie was broken suddenly by a cacophony of crows flying overhead, scolding us to action. Well, we'll be buzzard meat before we'll let some old crows tell us what for; when we knew they'd be the first ones to squawk it all around if something went wrong.

We were ready now, though, and we lifted the tire up and wheeled it to the edge. We watched it carefully so it wouldn't knock us over to the left and launch us over the cliff. We got it balanced and lined it up to let it go. And than with a goodly push we let loose of it. And it loosed! With all that weight it just shot down that hill with a fury. At first we started to run after it as we had with our normal tires, but quickly we skidded to a stop in amazement. This tire had clearly taken this challenge very seriously. It had barely gone 50 feet and already was going near 60 miles hour or so it seemed. It crashed through bushes without so much as a thank you; it slapped down saplings without a care, and began leaping effortlessly over boulders. It seemed to be winged and when it approached 80, our exhilaration began to take on shades of foreboding. What had we let loose?

As it got farther into the distance, we began to hope that no one had wandered into the mine. There was no stopping this mad tire. As we watched now in almost panic, it would hit a small mound and launch into the air, not touching down again for 40 or more feet. It seemed to know just where to leap, just what to dodge, just what to mow over as it sped to the bottom. What a thrill to watch. But we all had the same thought stirring. Surely when it hit the flat at the bottom, headed across the little meadow it would run out of steam before entering the woods. Wouldn't it? It shot down the last leg of the hill and entered the meadow with plenty of breath left and we could see it wouldn't stop. *It was going to make the woods.* Surely the trees would stop it, if it entered the woods. All those tall sturdy ponderosas with their progeny growing thick round-about would wrestle it to the ground, if not block it altogether, right?

We could see that as it reached the far end of the meadow it was tiring a bit. First it weebled a little, and then it wobbled. The tire then weebled a little more and wobbled once again. Than it weebled an even bigger weeble and wobbled a really big wobble; then it just weebled and wobbled until we were sure it had weeble wobbled itself out. With a last little weeb and wob it certainly looked like it had. With what feeble energy it had left, it surly couldn't make it through the trees. Because if it did there was the fence and this was a very high-strung fence. And we knew that a very high-strung fence tends to complain loudly when struck with great force. We had seen cows try it. Every staple in the post near the offense would screech out in complaint and their screeching could be heard miles down the fence. Now high-strung fences are indignant enough when bovines chased with horseflies or horses chased by cow flies run into them, cry out loud enough, what with rusty staples hanging on for dear life; but we knew that to be insulted by a big rubber tire would be too much and the fence would cry out with passion. We did not want it to hit the fence. Even more, Dad would not want it to hit the fence. Which meant the fence, if hit, would certainly screech its loudest complaint, as to be sure Dad heard it.

It couldn't last though with enough energy to make it through the woods anyways we assured ourselves nervously. But what couldn't and wouldn't, did. It gave up its feeble weeble, stopped the wobble to a mere wob and weaved and wove itself through the trees with nary brushing one. By this time it was clean out of oomph but rolled on. It labored for every inch forward. But it did the unthinkable. It crept up to the fence and bumped into it and fell over.

Left at that everything would have been fine, but no. Little did we know that Dad had just walked down this fence line from the house to get an old piece of steel from off the old 36′ flatbed, and he turned, aroused by a crunching and crackling sound emanating from the woods. To his dismay, he saw a huge tire dragging itself towards him through the trees. It bumped into the fence, and the fence let out a shriek. The tire expired nearly at Dad's feet. He stood there a bit flummoxed. He looked about. What a shock, for there was nobody around.

And what about the fence, you ask? It had let out one of the loudest screeches it could muster. The sheer size and weight of the tire strained those fence staples to their utmost and they let Dad know it. We heard the shriek, so we raced down the hillside and through the woods as fast as we could so to tell our side of story, before the fence stretched things a bit as it was wont to do when it tried to get us in trouble. Upon our explanation, Dad could see that the almost impossible thing had happened and only left us with the admonishment of being more careful in the future.

That tire had traversed almost a quarter of mile with the most fantastic feats of athleticism ever witnessed and ended up at it goal, exhausted and completely tired.

ACCURACY

I threw a dirt clod and missed. I bent down again and got another one. Here they come. I throw another and missed again. I hurriedly bent down to pick up another and hurled it at the approaching fighter planes. I missed again as before.

These little aerobatic fighters were actually cliff swallows, which were darting around in the cool air of the evening. They were in the process of snatching mosquitoes and other bugs from the air. I was out in the back yard by the far end of the clothesline and as these little birds cavorted around the yard, they sped ever so close to me. I was firing at them as fast as I could muster up dirt clods. Here they come again.

I crouched down with my hand loaded with another clod and when the group of them swung into range, I cocked my arm and fired away. A soft *pow* and a little puff of dust and a little bird tumbled ungracefully from the sky. I was shocked. Never had I or any of my siblings been able to hit one of these little birds. They were so small, so fast, and flew so erratically that it was only the sport of throwing at them as they darted and flitted around that lent it to being so much fun. In fact, we weren't supposed to be hitting these swallows. Dad had made it clear what critters were fair game and which were off- limits; these little guys were definitely off limits.

In shocked amazement, I picked up the little guy and stroked his feathers. Lucky for him, and me, his injury was slight, and he began to be restored to his wits. He struggled a little and I spread his wings to see if his dainty limbs were broken. They weren't. As he struggled harder, I just soaked in the beauty of his shimmering bluish and green feathers, his handsome shape which made him such a versatile flyer and his tiny feet which I could barely feel. He got impatient now and was eager to be off, so I launched him into the air and he skyrocketed out of the yard.

Boy was I glad. Dad's reasoning abilities were not less than most Dads, and if he found a downed flyer of such consummate skill, grounded in the vicinity of a 12-year-old boy, the two would be undoubtedly connected. Fortunately, the dirt clod being soft splattered well enough when it hit the bird and he escaped unharmed. I, too, escaped harm but not without some chagrin.

How could it be that when you have reached the age when you understand most of the things you need to know, given there might be a few small particulars your elders might be able to enlighten you on, that life throws a curve? How is it that when you know, for certainty that what you are about to do cannot happen, and therefore you do it with utmost concentration and, it happens? Confused?

Well a case in point is just what I related to you. I knew I was not supposed to injure swallows. I knew I would get in great trouble if I did. I knew that I couldn't hit these fast tiny swerving targets. I knew soft dirt clods were unreliable projectiles. Put it all together and you get to the perfectly logical conclusion, fire away at will because nothing bad can happen. So I did. And what did it get me? It got me a whole heap of bewilderment and a scrape with trouble.

Another case in point happened on a nice summertime sunny day. I entered the house, went back by the beds and lowered a bow from the gun rack. Well, the rack was made by Leo to be a gun rack, but right now it just served as a bow rack. Yes, the bow I had was a light wooden bow. It had about a 25-pound draw weight. I had just been raised to the responsible age for a bow, although I still kept my trusty slingshot on my hip. Jeremy had passed the bow down to me after he had gotten permission from Leo to use his 40-pound recurve Bear bow whenever he wanted;

Leo now sported a 60-pound Bear bow he had recently purchased.

I ran outside with the bow and after I got up into the pasture, I started shooting at anything I fancied. Now shooting at something is not the same thing as hitting it. These mountain lions, bears and raccoons had disguised themselves as clumps of grass, gopher mounds, and tumble weeds. They were in no mortal danger of expiring before their appointed hour. By the time I was called in for dinner, I was tired and my enthusiasm was a bit diminished. Hitting something I was aiming at seemed a wholly lost cause. It was with this attitude that I arrived on the back porch. I pulled up onto the porch and was ready to turn to the door to open it when an empty pie tin caught my eye. It was lying somewhat lazily in the late sun. It had given up some leftovers to the birds and seemed to have no place to go. This was not an ordinary pie tin. It was of a thicker aluminum than most and it had red sides. Maybe the sun had warmed it a bit and made it a little saucy because it caught my eye and it demanded attention.

For a split second I was tempted to shoot at this inviting target. Just a split second and then it was gone. It returned the second half of the split second with a little dare. "You couldn't hit it any ways," it seemed to say. *Oh yea*, now my pride was stung. Now the pie tin knew as well as I that Mom was in the habit of using this tin a lot and it was certainly not to be ruined. That is why it had to marshal temptation as its conspirator. After my pride was stung it knew I was weakened and right before I turned to enter the door it slung another arrow. "You never hit even one thing you aimed at out there," it cried out, "so there is no way you would ever hit this time." Now the tin had a point there. I hadn't hit anything yet. I began to reason that indeed there was no possibility of me ever hitting it, and so what the problem? Just one last little shot right before supper to finish off the evening I reasoned. Now something should have told me something was not going to turn out just right, for here I was reasoning with temptation, and we all know that when we get that far, temptation's probably going to win the argument. But reason I did and it all added up to this. There was no way that however I concentrated, however steady I was, I was going to hit that pie tin. The thought certainly didn't register any discomfort. It rested in perfect ease as it saw my will weakening. Thus weakened, I did the most unreasonable reasonable thing. I turned, knocked the arrow and raised my bow. I drew back in the most Robin Hoodish way I knew how and let fly the shaft. In shocked amazement, I watched the arrow fly true and it pierced the side of the pie tin.

Stunned, I walked off the porch. I couldn't have hit it. I didn't want to hit it. I didn't really even want to shoot at it. Now what was I to do? I wish with all my heart I had done the noble thing and told on myself. But I didn't. I did the cowardly thing and hid it behind the cookbook amongst the pots and pans in the pantry; and I wished the whole sorry trouble would pass. It did. I don't remember how. But I do remember thinking how did that ever happen, when it was virtually inconceivable given the circumstances that it could.

Maybe those should have been missed adventures instead of misadventures. Then nothing or anything would have gotten hurt or damaged. On the other hand, there would be a few blank pages in this book and that wouldn't do. Every page has its purpose. Something can be learned from it. So it is in a book, so it is in life. It makes a better book, and it makes a better life.

Hear Them Roar

It was the kind of summer day that lent one to musing. You know, it was kind of hot, and kind of humid. So musing we were doing, Jeremy and I. We were perched atop a hill in the old mine behind our house. Not a really tall hill, just one of two pushed up against each other. Mine tailings these hills were, now overgrown and pushed just high enough by the miners so we could see over the trees that divided the mine from the farm. From atop these, we could look out over the farm and the fields beyond.

A gnat flew erratically around our heads a few times as if confused. Did I hear it nattering to itself as it flew laps around our heads? Gnats natter? Hmm? Chicks' chirp, chimps' chatter, bovines' bellow, so I guess gnats might natter. But if they do natter, do they natter when they knit? And if nattering when they knit, do these nattering gnats knit in knickers or bockers, or both? If in both, do the knitted goods knitted by Knickerbocker gnats look different than just knickered gnats knitted goods? Possibly for gnats it all ends up as knots anyway. But does it matter? Really?

I wonder. And so I mused.

So... I pulled up my knees and wrapped my arms tightly around my lower legs and pulled them up close so I could rest my chin on my knees. Settling this way, I began to ponder the question of knitting gnats, but was jerked from this lazy reverie by a distinct rumble in the distance. It grew louder, quickly so, causing me to jerk my head up and look at Jeremy. He had obviously heard it, too, as his eyes were growing bigger as the roar became louder. We both whipped our heads to the left just in time to see two fighter jets burst into sight just over the treetops about a quarter of a mile away. They shot out over the farmland at just under the speed of sound and traversed the fields before us, flying not much higher than the hill we were perched on. The deafening roar seemed to take our breath away as we watched open mouthed. So close, and so low were they that we could distinctly see the pilots in their helmets.

They seemed for one minute to be frozen in time and we half expected the pilots to turn and salute as they streaked on by. So astonished we were at the suddenness of the noise, the speeding planes, and quickness with which they disappeared across the fields to our right, that our mouths had no time to close. We just stood there gaping for a moment as our jangled nerves began to un-jungle. These gray fighter jets, with some red painted on them, seemed almost mythical in the manner of their appearance and disappearance; it took a moment to sink in. As we sat there in stunned amazement, did I hear the gnat whip on by in a beeline for the bushes? Did these jets jangle him, too? I couldn't be sure I heard him natter, thought I might have caught a weak nitter at least, but I knew for sure that this gnat was definitely in a twit as no respectable gnat would beeline. Beeline?! He's a gnat nitwit. They gnatline. Excuse me. Gnats are very touchy you see, and get very annoyed especially when being written about.

Nittering gnats or not, we jumped up and raced home to tell Dad about our jets. Unfortunately, he was in the house and didn't see the planes and so couldn't tell us what kind they were, but he was able to tell us what they were doing. This was still during the Cold War with the Soviet Union and we thought this might have something to do with the Russians.

No, Dad said. These jets were just showing off.

They were doing a flyby for one of our neighbors. The neighbor worked the swing shift as a civilian at the airbase. The airbase was located a few miles west of town and these Air Force buddies would try to shake this neighbor out of bed with their thunderous noise. I don't know if it worked, but I do know it left our gnat beelining it to the bushes. Jeremy and I plopped down on the grass to rest. I couldn't help to again ponder if knitting gnats natter. I asked Jeremy;

"Do you think knitting gnats natter?"

"What?" he asked, looking at me as if I were crazy.

"What do you mean, do knitting gnats natter? Whoever heard of a knitting gnat?"

He had a point there. Who had heard of knitting gnat? They're pretty small, so it would be kind of hard to actually see one in the act. I suppose if they did they wouldn't go noising it all about, so probably you wouldn't actually see or hear one. But the philosophical question still remained, and I pushed on warming to the topic.

"Well take that little gnat as he buzzed around our heads. Should we really say he buzzed. Bees buzz, not gnats. As he whined about our heads it sure sounded like he was complaining. Complaining is good enough to be nattering in my book. So *yes* we can say gnats natter. But whether they knit when they natter, that's really the question."

"No, the question really is if this is chatter matter," Jeremy chimed in; he, too, was warming up to the fun.

"You see, if this is not chatter matter, than any chit-chat we have of the matter doesn't matter and whether gnats knit, just becomes chitter chatter. Now as the larger question of whether knitting gnats would knit in Knickerbockers would probably depend on clime or condition. Norway gnats would be more inclined to knit knickerbockers than knit *in* knickerbockers as knickerbockers only reach to knees and a Knickerbocker gnat in Norway would probably freeze. But I do think a Knickerbocker gnat would be freer as to his knees and therefore what he knit would be a little different than the non-knickered gnat."

Now I could see his point there. "But on the other hand" I had to point out, "Knickerbockered knee free gnats knees in Norway would knock in the freeze, thereby making knitting nary impossible."

"True, true," Jeremy muttered, "but I don't think this is chatter matter because we don't know if gnats in Norway are knickered or not as to social position or age as it was in this country naught but a century ago."

"That would require some research" I concuured.

Well we had great fun along these lines about Knickerbockered gnats knitting and nattering, chittering and chattering and trailed off into our own reverie again. But it wasn't for long. We were coaxed from our reverie by a gentle but deep rumble. Could it be we wondered?

At times we could see way off in the distance to the south of us B-52 bombers and C-130 tankers circling in their flight patterns. A few times for reasons unknown to us, their flight patterns would be modified and these tankers and bombers would be sent to the north of town. This would sometimes put them directly over our heads, and sure enough, it now did. They came towards us from the distance and soon were upon us.

What a sight. And what noise. The six huge jet engines of the B-52s blanketed the landscape with a deafening roar. They traversed the sky so low that we thought it seemed these flying steel behemoths could be hit by a well-placed slingshot rock hurled from our weapons. I think the pilots thought so, too. A few times they would rock their planes from side to side as if to give salute. This friendly wave was to assure us that they were friends and would certainly not want to be fired upon by patriotic youngsters with sling-shots. They were well aware that another giant had been taken down by a boy with a slingshot not many centuries before.

Well we jumped up and down, waving and shouting at them as they roared over our heads. We fired our slingshots at them. Maybe we hit them. Couldn't be sure, would have been awfully hard to hear the rock ping against the side of a B-52 amidst all their noise, but one couldn't be too sure. They only made one pass this time and were gone. It was pretty good evidence that we'd scared 'em after all this excitement, but we couldn't muse anymore and went into the house.

These giant planes had many smaller friends and sometimes they would come our way, too. They would usually swarm from the south without warning. Mostly it seemed those times were at our dinner hour.

But first, imagine a covey of quail. If you can't, I'll help you. When quail crouch from danger, they do so in a group called a covey. They sit in a circle facing out, with all their little tails touching. That way if a marauding coyote or other predator gets too close, they launch themselves in all directions in a burst of noise and flapping wings. Since each is facing out from each other in a circle, they can burst forth from that center point without getting entangled with each other.

Well, a dinner table for 15 children is much the same as a covey. It's only different in three important ways. First, it's called a family not a covey, secondly, sitting is the preferred posture, not crouching, and lastly but most significantly, all the faces are turned inward, tails out. Remember, rapid transport from a central location without entanglement is the purpose of the design of the covey. The design of the family trough leads to the opposite ending. This is how it happens.

A low faint rumble is heard by one of the brood. Their jaw ceases to chew. Their eyes grow bigger as the sound grows stronger. When suddenly, "The jets are coming." They shout. And they launch themselves from their chair.

This initial shout and launch effort occasions the same response in the rest off the assemblage. The whole table erupts from the eating repartee as all scramble to get up and out the back door. But since this is a family at dinner, and not a covey, it is not an orderly transport. Since all are facing in, everybody's legs get entangled with each others' legs and the legs of the chairs, as they try to turn around to escape from the table. That's a lot of legs to get mixed up. Some of the chairs would run nearly to the door in the vain thought that they had a boy's legs, and some boy would crash to the ground trying to run on wooden legs. When all this leg confusion got figured out, the family would spurt out through the door to see the fast-approaching jets, while leaving behind a disarrayed line of chairs stretching from the table nearly to the door. Two, three, sometimes more, needle-nosed delta-wing fighter jets from the Air Force base would streak towards us at only a few thousand feet. Then right over our pasture they would shoot straight up like rockets, sometimes turning barrel rolls as they climbed towards the heavens. The deafening, thundering roar of engines would shake our bodies and the ground around. As the jets would become little more than dots way up there in the blue sky, they would mysteriously go over the top of an imaginary mountain and come screaming back down toward the earth.

Arching much too closely to the ground, we would stare in wonder and apprehension as the pilots pulled their planes from their dive and leveled off to shoot off towards the north. And then we would wait, and wait, and sometimes have to wait some more, but invariably, someone one would hear a slight rumble. We would look eagerly to the north, the south, the east, where are they? Then with an ever-increasing roar, those sneaky pilots would shoot out from behind the trees from the west, straight over our heads and we would begin hollering, screaming and yelling

"After Burners!" "After burners!" And most often they would treat us to what we loved best: firing up their afterburners.

The jet engine was mounted just under the tail and right when they pulled up to shoot up to the heavens, a streak of fire would burst out of the jet engine, and as the planes shot up, we could look straight up into their belly and see the orange-red cauldron of heat and flame, as it blasted the jet ever faster into the wild blue yonder. This extra boost was facilitated by a special compartment of the jet engine, which would kick into action if the plane needed an extra push to get it out of a tight spot with an enemy. This it did by capturing and igniting poorly burnt jet fuel as it left the tail of the jet. Thus, this is aptly named 'after-burner'. We loved to see this spectacular show of fire and thunder, as they stormed the heavens. So close, so loud, so fiery they would be. Then, in a flash, they were but little fiery dots in the sky, and then silence. We would listen a little more and then turn back into the house.

It wasn't easy to crowd back into the house to resume dinner. First, we had to do a leg check. No chair legging it for the door, no child thumping around with a wooden leg and no table leg bent at the knee. Good.

With the roar of the jets faded away we commenced eating and talking once more. I hope the roar of the jets have faded a bit for you, too. You'll need your ears for the next tale.

Dogs, Dogs, Dogs

Dogs are man's best friend. You've heard this been said. I've heard this been said. But did the dogs hear this said? Well, they might have heard it said, but did it form their character such that it affirmed the truth of the dictum? The evidence suggests not. The evidence quite firmly suggests otherwise. The fine words fell on the ears of dogs the same throughout our fair land I suppose, but not always with the result what we would wish: a companion trusty and true. But on others it fell on a hard soul and did not penetrate. Enemy in man is what they saw. Walking upright on two legs? Enemy. Legs. To be bitten. Two legs on a boy, those legs on a bike, those legs were to be bitten while on the bike. It all added flavor, spice to life, and the excitement of the chase.

And that was where most country boys stood in the minds of the dogs that patrolled the county roads in front of the farmer's houses. It was the ilk of the two Doberman pinchers times 10 that patrolled the roads leading to the house where I got my first job.

I was 12 years old. I was taking over the responsibilities of a large garden that a kindly widow woman, Mrs. King needed caring for. I was taking over for Jeremy, as he was moving up to greater things, like working for a local farmer in his haying operation. Dogs were always a menace to boys on bikes. Some dogs were more of a menace than others. Some figured their duty was the protection of the family farm or to just put a little fear in the passing boy. These type of dogs would just sort of escort any boy on down the road with a 'kinda like to know ya, but keep on moving' attitude. Others thought it was necessary to show a little tooth, raise the boy's blood pressure a bit, and make his trip go by very fast. And others took their duty very seriously and would actually bite any leg they could catch.

The biters were a big problem, even when the

dog was little. That the big dog biters were trouble is understood. But the little biters, although being little, seemed to elicit practically the same adrenal response as the big biters. For those of you who have never had the pleasure of being dog biter bait, the following illustrations might help for you to feel what we felt. Some parallel illustrations will make clear the point.

For a little dog biter and the effect it has on a bike rider is very much like this.

Have you ever see a grown up all dressed up for work in a nice pressed white shirt, cool as cucumber, with a mosquito loose in their car? Seventy miles an hour down the road they cruise and suddenly their hands are off the wheel, flailing madly around in panic, swatting and swapping in sheer terror, as they try to avoid a tiny little bite. The car swerves madly to and fro, the mosquito whines and zips around, and either the mosquito ends up squashed on their beautiful white shirt or the car heads into the ditch, across the fields and heading for the trees; the driver still unawares to the bigger picture, is focused and frantically trying to locate the rascally bug. See how that little bug elicits such a huge response. Well that's like the little dogs when they attack a biker. There's a huge response to avoid a small bite.

Now imagine the pandemonium that ensues when it's a hornet loose in the car. That's like a big dog biter.

Sheer madness commences. The wild-eyed, screaming, and flailing driver careens madly down the road. His hands free of the wheel, he tries to open the windows, swat at the bee, and unfasten the seat belt so he can run around in the car. He does everything but drive. The angry buzz of the bee and imminent sting prods him on. All reason and safety is discarded in his mad attempt to escape. Car wreck or bee deliverance, whichever comes first will be the result. All these fantastic antics to avoid a sting are startling. To avoid the sting they risk a 68 car pile-up and possibly death. Well, that's like a biker avoiding a big dog biter.

So now that I have described the canine mentality as regards to boys on bikes, I must introduce one of a few of Dad's home remedies meant to alleviate some of life's perils. They will figure in a few of these adventures. I will introduce them when a remedy is called for. One is called for now and deals with this problem of biting dogs. Might seem a little harsh to the squeamish, but it was meant to keep boy and his leg attached in a long and loving relationship.

Dad proffered that he had heard at work, some men talking who said if you mixed some ammonia in water and placed this in a squirt bottle you could spray this in the dog's eye. The resulting sting would take the fight out of the dog as you rode clear and there would be no lasting harm to the dog. Lasting harm you say, pneumonia certainly does harm you over time, even unto death. I said ammonia, not bottled pneumonia. See?

Well, I had mentioned above about a pair of Doberman pincers; it wasn't an honorable mention, you might have noticed, they didn't deserve as much. No, these two dogs had become nemeses of the first degree. They had harassed Jeremy and me the whole preceding summer as they patrolled the road leading to our swimming hole and also where Jeremy worked. They were truly mean and we could see that serious injury would result if they got a hold of us.

Now, I had gotten tired of being harassed by all these dogs as I set about adventuring and resolved to end it once for all. These Dobermans had to be dealt with, especially since I now carried a small gash on my ankle from a little dog biter that still smarted. And it was just a little puff piece that flew out at me as I struggled up a hill and got a fang on me before my adrenals could kick in and propel me from danger. It was a good indication of what it would really feel like if bitten by these German war machines.

So today I filled a squirt bottle with water and added ammonia from Mom's cleaning arsenal in a mix about six times stronger than recommended by Dad. I had Doberman pincers on my mind and resolved to keep them off my leg.

Thus was I armed when I set out to Mrs. King's. I pedaled with an air of nonchalant confidence as I pedaled up the driveway. I turned right and began down to the county road. I could see the full three-quarters of the mile down to the next road where I would turn left. I could see that no Dobermans were patrolling there. I pedaled that length with deterio-rating nonchalance, but confidence still residing. I had ammonia water I reminded myself. I turned left. I could see the next 200 feet to the right turn I next anticipated. But there was still no sign of danger. Apprehension began to fight with confidence. As they fought, they bumped into the sides of my stomach and little butterflies started to make merry there. I made it to the right turn onto the gravel road with no sight of these German killers. I was right smack in the middle of their territory now, and if they spotted me from their yard, they would be on me in a flash. My idea was to gain as much speed as possible, so that when they did see me I would have a fighting chance to get by them and out of their territory before I were caught.

I hove into my pedals with a heart and had a good clip going when the mad roar of their barks shattered the silence. All in the first half of a split second I looked ahead about 100 yards, and spied the left gravel turn I wanted to make, which would take me the next 100 yards to Mrs. King's. In the second half of the split second, gravel spewed from my rear tire as I laid into my pedals with a will. The dogs were after me. They gained on me so fast I felt as if I stood still and it seemed that in the next moment they were upon me. Fear took a good grip on my Adam's apple as I glanced under my right shoulder at my pedal. There, not an inch from my ankle, were the curled back lips of the female pincer; her wicked teeth bared, straining to get my ankle, and not 6 inches behind, her mate was growling in anger. Both of their legs were churning the gravel into dust in their frenzy to get me.

It was an all-out race of life or death. I don't to this day even know how I had under these circumstances managed to muster a little courage, for frightened, he had slipped down into my ammonia bottle. I rallied him up and I roused him to action. I let go of my right handlebar where I had gripped in my hand the squirt bottle. I twisted around and down and aimed right into her eyes and let her have it good in both eyes. What happened next is almost too horrendous to describe. She let out a howl of rage and pain. Her eyes turned red with killer rage. Malicious lips sprang back to reveal the most wicked looking mouth of fang and fury I have ever seen. She sprang in desperation to grab my leg and she managed to hook one viscous eyetooth onto my pant leg. The male's snapping jaws tried to get at me over her back.

In the maelstrom, I could see what seemed was the whole German fighting machine in full force as these dogs really meant to kill me. I turned in mortal fear and grasped my right handlebar in a death grip and pedaled as furiously as all my powers could marshal. The dog's fang had ripped out one of my pant legs and she strove to get another bite. The male, now only inches away, sought not to be outdone by a female. But hell has no fury as a woman scorned and surely I was looking into the wailing and the gnashing of that infernal place. It seemed like an eternity as we raced down that gravel road. My eyes were fixed on the turn I wanted to make. It seemed as though I were running in water, so slowly did that turn approach, but suddenly I was upon it. I cranked my handlebars over and laid my bike low to make that turn on the fly. Only too late did I realize that I was flying way too fast to make that turn on gravel. My bike slid into the turn and then straight over side of the ditch. I hit the bottom of the ditch still going like 60 miles per hour.

Now this wasn't a little wimpy sissified ditch meant to handle a trickle of discarded wandering water. No, this was a man-sized country ditch as deep as my shoulders and had rocks the size of oranges dotting the whole bottom of it. Well, I flew into that ditch as I was saying; and I never let off pedaling as I continued to pedal furiously down this ditch towards Mrs. King's. Dodging some and hitting others of those rocks, my bike was like a jackhammer under me and I was nearly beaten to pieces. Finally it penetrated my fear-besotted mind that the dogs were no longer after me. I don't know if they just stopped in utter amazement as they saw me sailing into that ditch in desperation or they had reached the end of their territory. But I pulled myself up out of that ditch by Mrs. King's.

Dog less, beleaguered and breathless, I pulled up to a stop, to gather about myself the wits that sheepishly had crawled back to me. Securing them again to my person for use at a later date, I looked down and saw that to my surprise, when I had re-grasped the right handlebar, I had clenched the water bottle so tightly and squished it so decidedly between my hand and the handlebar that it was nothing but a mangled piece of worthless plastic. Being not a little non-plussed over that, a little more of my dignity was subtracted when I realized that I shouldn't even have attempted to make that last turn. I could have continued straight on the dirt road and sailed on by it; gone around a country block and come in on the other side of Mrs. King's.

Whoo! Whee! A little peaked, I pushed my bike the rest of the way to her yard.

Sitting a bit limply at her table, I related my adventure to Mrs. King. She fortified me with lemonade whenever I pushed the glass towards her for more. You will, I hope, withhold too much blame as I must relate, I had not two, but three or four glasses and at least as many cookies, before my spine began to stiffen and color return to my pale face. Fortified with these restoratives, I regained enough strength to get up from the table and go out to the garden. Potato bugs and cutworms had better watch out. Seeing what ammonia water did to the Dobermans made me think, maybe I ought to try the long- term weapon of pneumonia and not ammonia on the bugs.

And the dogs, they disappeared not too long after this encounter. They had bitten a neighbor boy's leg really good one day, unprovoked. The people moved away. As to Dad's home remedies, turn the page and read about me and the Cayenne..

THE CAYENNE PEPPER CAPER

Many different health initiatives were making their rounds when I was a youngster and one of these caught the attention of my Dad. This was an herbal-based regimen. Dad researched it, and armed with his knowledge bought some of them and set about an herbal regimen. Amongst the various exotic names that attached themselves to the different bottles of herbs was one called cayenne. Not a particularly unattractive name, no, but not really attractive enough to write home about. That is, if I were away from home that is. I wasn't, so didn't, but still wouldn't. Now it could call itself cayenne if it really wanted, I wasn't acquainted with it, so it could go about meeting new friends with that name if it wanted. I didn't mind. But I shouldn't have been quite as cavalier about this fellow cayenne as I was soon to find out.

The claim to fame of this here fellow was that it was good for the blood. If your blood was still in your body you ingested him. This would purify your blood. If your blood was spilling out of your body it would coagulate it. Stop it. See. Simple. Blood ailments? This here fellow was there to help. I had overheard Dad talking to someone that during the war this pepper was applied to wounds with healthful results. It sounded good to me. Why would one want details?

Now I suffered from the distress of a frequently bleeding nose. At about 10 years old, Mom took me to the doctors and they cauterized it. It helped some but not a lot, and my beak continued to leak. It was quite handy for sympathy at times. Get a bump on the nose when wrestling with one of my brothers and the floodgates would open up. There was enough blood there to look as if I had been mauled by a bigger than average Alaskan grizzly bear. Quite irritating, though, when playing football or basketball and having to stop playing to take care of it.

There was one consolation. One of my mountain man heroes was John Colter, the white man who discovered Yellowstone National Park. Well, on the way to discovering this pearl, he was a bit distracted from his pursuit when a pursuit much dearer to his heart at the time needed immediate attention. You see, cadres of Indians bent on his death were after him. They had just filled his trapping buddy with arrows and John saw no attraction in having it repeated in him. The Indians had captured him, stripped him of his clothes and moccasin's, gave him a few seconds head start and said *run*! Well, he knew better than to ask how fast and he got down to serious business. A large river was six miles ahead and he knew if there was any chance of survival, he must make the river. He ran over the prickly pear and stones until his feet went numb. Still 100 yards from the river he could hear a brave breathing in tortured breath draw nearer and nearer up behind him. Suddenly his own tortured breathing burst his nose wide open and the blood flowed in torrents from his nostrils. Sensing he would be impaled from behind any moment from the approaching brave, he stopped suddenly and spun around. The brave was so startled by the blood-drenched horror that he saw, that it caused him to stumble. When he drew up to throw his spear to run Colter through that stumble cost him his life and saved Colter's. John grabbed the spear from the ground and in turn killed the brave as he leapt to grab him. Never before, as I know, was a bloody nose responsible for changing the course of history. But it did.

That's not the end of the nose bleeds and Indians; oh no, as you will see they got their revenge.

Having heard that cayenne could remedy all things bloody, I set about to elicit his aid. Now normally the taking of this herb was through a capsule. There was powdered herb in each capsule and a person would ingest one orally as so prescribed. But I was using all the incredible knowledge I had acquired at this advanced age of 13, discovered that I could pry this capsule apart and empty out the contents. With that wisdom I had reasoned like this. If cayenne was such a hot commodity that it could staunch blood than surely, some dutifully applied into a bloody nose would do its magic and in seconds the blood would stop its trek out of the body, stiffen up and behave; and I would be off on my merry adventuring.

Well, not so fast. I didn't know that the cayenne was the first cousin of the Cheyenne, the Indian tribe noted for its ferociousness in battle. Well that was the connection in my young mind when I heard the word cayenne. The words sounded so much alike and when I saw them spelt they looked so much alike, I always wedded those two words in my mind with the Indians. Well, that's the way it was, and the Cheyenne decided to set up camp in my nose with the cayenne, when I dumped it in there.

It happened like this. One hot day as I was out hunting ground squirrels with my bow and arrow I got a bloody nose. I hurried to the house, one finger pushing hard on the side of my nose to staunch the flow. I had no time for this I figured, and thought what a perfect time to apply the new remedy I discovered so I could get right back outside. I found the cayenne in its bottle in the cupboard and plopped down on the nearest bed at hand. I lay down and I took a capsule into my hand. Putting it up in front of my face, I carefully pried open the capsule, careful not to spill one grain of this powerful stuff. I wanted the full dose in order to get this nosebleed over with quickly.

I had to do this fast as I had let go of the pressure on my nose and the blood was starting to flow down my throat. Balancing the open capsule in my right hand and opening the bleeding nostril with the other, I proceeded with haste to dump the whole capsule of cayenne pepper into my nose. The result was less than satisfying and a whole lot more painful.

A searing, burning pain lit into my nose almost instantaneously. I shot nearly 2 feet straight up off of the bed in mortal pain. The pain burst into my sinuses like a bomb going off and lit up fireworks throughout my head. I leapt up from the bed in agony with the unfortunate consequence of pouring the blood out of my nose onto the bed and floor. To stop it, I instinctively pinched my nose with great pressure, as the blood seemed to be gushing in earnest, trying to escape this blasted inferno. This was the last thing one wants to do when one has a nose full of pepper. It just pushed that pepper more firmly into every last nook and cranny of my cranium. I rushed to the bathroom trying to think of what I was going to do with this raging inferno in my head. Unfortunately the Cheyenne's had come to stay and were doing battle in my nose. Bows, tomahawks, spears and knives were applied indiscriminately to the inside of my noggin. John Colter having escaped from the Indians' bloodthirsty grasp, through the fright of a bloody nose had made these Indians bound and determined to take out their revenge in my nose. Had I known that cayenne had such a hot reputation and such savage relatives, I never would have invited him into my nose in the first place.

I lurched in pain into the bathroom and bent over the bathtub to let the blood and pepper flow out. And out it did flow, torrents of it. I frantically splashed cold water over my face. The pain was so intense it nauseated me and I had trouble trying to keep the rest of my insides from flowing out in hot pursuit. I bent over the tub, stunned into inaction by the intensity of the hurt. My whole noggin seemed to be on fire. I doused rivers of ice cold well water over my head and in my face until I gained a bit of sanity through the fog of pain to do something. Fortunately this raging inferno, hurting like heck, was of shorter duration than hell, and ended up being what seemed like an eternity in purgatory.

Fortunately purgation ends, it eventually began to subside and the last of the Cheyenne's followed the cayenne out. I once again pressed my nose to stop the flow. This time the pressure seemed to do some good, and the pain subsided to a dull, deep throb. I had no choice but to keep my finger tightly pressed to my offending snout. There I hunched for awhile as my eyes settled back into their sockets, the tears slowed their flow and my nose began to shrink to a respectable Roman patrician's size. I gingerly released my finger hoping that no more cayenne was going to chase my innards out. I had been delivered a savage blow to my nose, so I set myself to washing the gallons of blood that should have been in my veins, down the drain. After I was done, I got a wet washcloth and applied it to my nose. I wandered outside and lay perfectly still on the lawn trying to let the remaining pain subside. It took hours. Days later my upper nose remained tender and it took almost a week to get back to normal. My nose still bled on occasion after that, but I never called the cayenne back. Better to let them powwow with the Cheyenne.

And I think the pepper might have seared my brain a little because I wasn't through trying home remedies as interpreted by me. You read about ammonia and now cayenne. Did I tell you about onions and buttermilk? No? Well, you'll have to wait until I was a little older as I had to.

Errant Snowballs

"Ouch!" I hollered as a snowball from Jake plowed into my left ear. I bent down with my already numb hands and packed a ball as tightly as I could and tried to paste Jeremy as he was attempting to blindside Tristan. That was the way it was if we boiled out of the car on a snowy day after school. We were all full of energy and to be released into a wintry wonderland with good packing snow was an irresistible invitation to get into a snowball fight. Everyone was fair game whether they liked it or not. Generally there were no teams. It was a free for all. You just ran, ducked, and scooped up snow to form another pro-jectile, and looked around for the juiciest target. You had to act fast, though, as at least two of the other siblings were bound to have had let a snowball fly at you while you were busy loading up. The snowball that plowed into your teeth was the worst. A clout on the ear was always a smarter. And snow cascading down your neck after a snowball clobbered you on the back of the head always made us dance around like we had ants in our pants, as we clawed down our shirts to try to get it out.

There were two rules that were impressed upon us both literally and figuratively concerning our snowball fights. There was the spoken word from Dad and there was the imprint on our behinds, which kept free interpretation of the spoken word from gaining traction.

The one was:

Thou shalt not throw snowballs towards the house; even if one of your siblings, in a craven act of coward-ice, would retreat to its confines after plastering you with a perfectly thrown projectile.

The other was:

Thou shalt not throw snowballs at the cars: again, even if one of your nemeses let fly to your eye with an ice ball, and then dives into that windowed enclosure for safety from retaliation. Now mind you, if I sought the refuge of the house after say, pasting Tristan a good one, that would be considered a masterstroke of keen intelligence combined with quick thinking to preserve one's delicate existence in this world. But if

Tristan or Jake, or Jeremy would duck for the house, I think you can all see what a cowardly act that would be.

There was good reason, of course, for these dictates of Dad's. Both of these enclosures were sprinkled liberally with windows, and if any windows or doors were inopportunely open at the time when a snowball was sailing towards them, it would enter unceremoniously in and damage whatever they struck or leave water damage when they would melt into the surroundings as an unwanted guest. Now if the window or door was shut when the snowball chased the boy or girl target, then the glass would shriek its indignation, shatter itself into bits, fall tinkling to the floor and leave its jagged up turned hands protruding from the windowpane, as if to say "Now look what you've done."

No, the house was for living in, and the car for conveying, neither were to be used for forts.

But alas, one fine sunny day, after a snowstorm the day before, the snow lay somewhat sodden on the ground. This confluence of events lent itself wonderfully for snowball fights. The snow was heavy and malleable, the air was somewhat warm by winter standards and the spirits were high on account of the sun. Tristan, Peter, Cecilia and I were throwing at each other and anybody else who would venture out to do animal chores, and sometimes some of the older ones making the rounds would pelt us with snowballs and then go about their business.

Meanwhile, unbeknownst to us, Dad had set up

shop in the living room. In it he had cut large sheets of particle board into planks of which he was to build a very large shelf. Particle board as some of you may know is a partly man-made wood as it is sawdust compressed together with glue. The two are fused into a board with pressure and dried. Unlike planks cut from a tree and therefore solid wood, particle board is particularly susceptible to water damage. Water will very quickly make it swell and crumble, making it useless in no time.

So inside we have Dad in quiet concentration, measuring, sawing, gluing and nailing together this huge shelf made out of particle board.

Outside we have a large assortment of half unwrapped kids, throwing, screaming, laughing, and crying, and running.

Inside and outside are not to be mixed.

But on account of a running and looking for a juicy target to plaster with a snowball, my judgment got impaired. Tristan and I were standing, panting and chattering to each other after having fired off a volley of snowballs at Jeremy and Cecilia. They had subsequently disappeared around the corner of the house and we were for a moment alone.

We had just bent down and were preparing new wet snow balls in order to launch another fusillade at are attackers, as they were sure to return with reinforcement from Jake and Rose. I was holding a particularly well made snowball in my hand when out from around the corner of the house shot Peter on the run, having been flushed out from behind the house from Jeremy and Cecilia as they disappeared from us. Tristan and I were standing about 15 feet from the house directly out the front door. We spotted Peter at the same time as he spotted us, and his eyes grew big as saucers when he spied us loaded up to plaster him. He did the only thing possible under the circumstances to avoid a barrage of wet snow. He streaked for the front door. The dictum "Thou shalt not throw at the house," flitted momentarily through my mind. But Peter's flight to the door was fleet and I had no more time than that flit to determine my choice. That's when good judgment fled. I cocked my arm and released that round, sloppy wet snowball. Timing had to be just right to catch Peter right before he flung the screen door open and twisted the knob of the front door to dive into safety.

Well, I stood frozen in incredulity as I saw timing unfold in what seemed like slow motion. As my snowball flew in a beautiful arc towards Peter, perfect to catch him on the fly as he dove for the door, their two trajectories were just perfect to collide with knifelike precision before the door. But wait, what is this? Just a moment before contact, Peter flings the screen door open, the snowball just misses that door as Peter than twists the knob of the front door and thrusts it open. The gap between him, the opening now unveiled into the house, and which his body did not block, could not have been but a few inches, but in horror I saw my snowball slide between Peter and the open door and enter the house without even a tip of the hat at the doorjamb. Ha! So he didn't have a hat; a quick flip of an ice chip could at least been attempted when entering the house uninvited at that clip.

No. Frozen in time, forever etched in my mind is the picture of Dad kneeling on the floor, one plank of particle board held up perpendicular to the floor, him bending over in concentration as he carefully applies a strip of glue. The snowball is now descending from its arc, flashing through the door and smashing full force into Dad's plank inches from his face. Wet snow splatters all over the living room. The remainder of my creation sticks momentarily on the plank and then slides down it, sort of sick like, to rest and pool on the floor. It seemed to be much like my soul. It, too, seemed to drain from my head, and trickle down into my heart sort of heavy like. It continued its crawl down my body till it seemed to puddle around my feet. Movement was impossible. Both Tristan and I were stunned. Dad rose slowly to his feet and we remained motionless.

There must have been a rush of thoughts and emotions that pushed for attention in Dad. We knew we had done something terribly wrong. He rose slowly from his position on the floor and walked to the door. He looked at us without anger and said quietly, "Which one of you boys did this?" I weakly raised my hand a little and said "I did." That was all. But I felt small. "I think you boys know better than that," and he turned and closed the door softly behind him.

And we did know better. And somehow in the wisdom that only Dad's have he saw that punishment was not necessary this time, although the crime was somewhat egregious. We walked away, chastened but not despondent, until the next invitation to adventure lifted our spirits and we set off again. With a little better foresight and more discipline surely?

Pump House Fire

Most farms in rural America drew or pumped their water from a well and ours was no exception. Dad had hand dug the well when we first moved out to the farm. I remember vividly as a 3 year old watching Dad lower himself 30 feet down into a 4-foot diameter hole. From there he would shovel some dirt into a pail and have Louisa, Elizabeth and Leo haul it up by pulling on a rope. Dad had run a rope through a pulley that hung from a tripod above the hole, down to an attachment on the bucket.

It was pretty scary for us, to see him slowly disappear, his voice getting ever more distant as he went lower and lower. We would peer nervously over the edge to watch him working down there. He looked so small and it was rather dark at the bottom. The hole he made was square like a mine shaft and shored on all sides with two by eight planks running up and down. He had wrapped a rope a couple of times around a steel pipe that traversed the top of the well, and he attached this to his belt. He held the other end in his hand, as he braced his feet against one wall and his back against the other and sort of slid down the hole. By continually flipping the rope he held in his hand, the loops around the pipe slid freely around as he went down, but if he slipped and lost his footing, instead of plunging to the bottom, he just pulled hard on the rope and it would tighten up immediately. The friction on the pipe would stop the slide of the rope and he would hang there until he was again braced, feet on one wall and back to the other. What was always incredible to us was his ability to pull himself back up with that rope. He virtually just climbed right back up with his arms. And this after having shoveled numerous buckets of dirt and shored the walls.

Now what does all this have to do with the pump house? Well, you wouldn't have a pump house if you didn't have a pump to house, and you wouldn't have a pump if you didn't have any water to pump. And where would you get the water to pump if you didn't have a well and at the bottom of the well, water. Well? Well, Daddy dug the water well upon which the pump house sat. And it was because of this sitting pump house that I was able to accidently almost burn it down.

You see, inside this pump house was also housed the pressure tank and located at the base of the tank was a water faucet. Something you didn't know because I haven't told you yet, is that this pump house was located about 80 feet east of the house out the back door. It also sat next to the cow pen. Because it sat so close to the cow pen, it was very easy to run a water hose from the faucet on the bottom of the tank to the cow watering trough. Minding, of course, the electric fence strung alongside the tank to keep the cows in. For a number of years from when I was about 10, it was my responsibility to water the cows and this was a daily activity.

At this age, a chore like this that cut about 20 minutes out of one's day seemed awfully onerous when one needs to play with trucks, hunt with the slingshot, capture bugs or one of the other august responsibilities that fall on one to keep the world on its proper course. Not infrequently, the cows would be bawling and mooing and a shout from somewhere would come, "Nathaniel, did you water the cows today?" And I would take off across the yard or from the field to see if my hope was right that they were setting up a fuss about some other bovine misfortune and not languishing from lack of water. Unfortunately the dry bottom of the trough told its tale and I would busy myself right quick to remedy the situation before their din would reach Dad. My tardiness to this task was not taken lightly and I preferred to set to it without the added incentive of a warmed over fanny.

Now in the wintertime this pump house needed to be heated to keep the water from freezing and bursting the water pipes. Dad accomplished this by mounting an electrical outlet about 5 feet high on the wall next to the door. A special light bulb made to give off heat called a heat lamp was plugged into this outlet and provided the needed heat. Now, the pump house was only about 6 feet high and about 8 feet square, not a large building by anybody's measure excepting mice. They considered it a very roomy mouse house and set up camp immediately. I didn't share this judgment of theirs and I fought a continuous battle to keep them out. I was losing this battle until the time when I inadvertently turned the pump house into a smokehouse.

It happened this a ways. In the room that was left in the pump house around the water pressure tank, we had gotten to storing items that we did not currently need for use. These included boxes of various sizes, some suitcases and some cardboard barrels packed with seasonal clothing and the like. All this cardboard made for wonderful recreational chewing by the mice, which made the contents of the containers imperiled. The cardboard would also make for the start of a wonderful fire.

Well one day in the early fall, when the temp had dropped to below freezing, the heat lamp was blazing away. Mom asked me if I could get her something out of one of the boxes. As chance would have it, it was not in one of the front boxes; no, I had to dig for it. Dug I did. But in my eagerness to burrow into the contents of these boxes I placed a blanket on top of a cardboard barrel, which was in turn stacked on its fellow. The height of the stacked barrels was just so that when I placed the blanket up out of the way, it sat a mere 2 inches from the face of the glowing heat lamp. I, of course, was oblivious to this and bored happily on my way. When I triumphantly caught the intended article, I put everything back in due order. I put everything back that is but the offending blanket. The light bulb glared with all its might directly on that blanket tucked so closely to it. I was blithely unaware of this heated exchange and duly closed the door when I was done. I took the article to Mom and went playing merrily on my way. An hour later, pandemonium broke loose.

"The pump house is on fire," someone shouts. There was a slight pause, then another. "The pump house is on fire!" Within seconds, a whole cacophony of cries of "The pump house is on fire! The pump house is on fire!" arises from every corner of the farm. From Jeremy in the plum tree to Jake on the swing, from Tristan in trouble, to Rose in the window arose such a din. From Damien and his dump trucks and Jessica in the bath, a general cry of alarm enveloped the peaceful landscape. I was playing in the woods when this eruption broke the balm, and I raced from the woods to see what the matter was. Sure as shooting, there was the blackest of smoke billowing from the top of the pump house door. I could not have been more astonished. Could it be? No. But yes. There was no getting around it. That building was definitely puffing. Did I say billowing? Yes, indeed I did, because it *was* billowing *and* puffing.

Fortunately Dad was home from work. And as opposed to the rest of the clan, who were too stunned by the shock to do anything but vigorously work the vocal pipes, Dad rushed to rescue the pump house.

When he flung the door open a huge cloud of acrid black smoke belched out at him. He ducked the thickest of it and so doing could look up into the pump house and see what the culprit was. On top of the cardboard barrels was a big brittle lump of what was left of the blanket. It spewed out hot smoke. Dad reached up and with gloved hands (fortunately he was already wearing them) grabbed the charred remains and flung it out onto the ground. And man was that the worst-smelling smoke ever smelt. A slight whiff was enough to burn the nostril and wretch the stomach. And by this time all our stomachs were gathered around to wonder and to wretch.

It was determined that because the pump house was so sealed up, the hot light could not actually cause the blanket to burst into flame, as there was not enough oxygen to be had, and so the light contented itself to trying to fry the blanket to a crisp. If any flame would have caught, what with all that cardboard and it being a wood building, the result would have been decidedly different. Where the building stood would have been a smoldering ash heap. As it was, the building stood. So did I.

But I sure paid for that awful oversight. You see, that blanket was made of acrylic, a kind of plastic, and when it burnt, it was practically lethal. Some chemical that had been released into the air by the burning blanket caused every piece of metal in that pump house to rust almost immediately. The hinges on the suitcases, all the nail heads, some wrenches, a hammer, pliers, anything metal that was exposed to that smoke was affected. But what was the worst for me, was that every time I opened that house to hook up the hose and water the cows I was met with a smell so foreign to any natural scent, it felt it would turn my insides out. So I resorted to holding my breath, wrenching the door open, trying to get the hose screwed onto the spigot, and leaping back out before having to take another breath. It worked a few times. The other times were spent trying frantically to hook a freezing snowy end of the hose onto a fouled up threaded spigot, all the time holding my breath as my hands became numb. It usually took a couple of times of reeling out of the pump house, blue in the face for lack of air, taking some gulps of frigid air and diving back in to wrestle that inflexible hose again. It didn't help if Tristan was out there. Pelted by snowballs or snow down my neck was the encouragement by him as I knelt on the floor with door wide open to frigid elements. This made the only thing out there that could melt, melt, and that was my sympathy for thirsty cows. Now this waning sympathy could have left some thirsty cows if the warming of my fanny by Dad's capable hands had not reinforced my weakening conscience. And so the cows got water. And I got rid of the mice.

Never again did I see a mouse so much as take a sidelong glance at that house again. Limburger cheese was probably the only cheese strong enough to penetrate the fried nostrils of the mice that survived the conflagration.

June and Cecilia

June was the first cow to grace the farm. A pretty Jersey, she could have walked right out of a country scene painted on the tins that contained Christmas cookies from relatives far away. Only she didn't. Oh, she strolled placidly enough from the trailer that Dad had loaded her into at the farm where we purchased her. She walked docilely at the end of the rope as Dad led her to her pen in the woods and she gave her pen and shelter an approving nod as she ambled through the gate. As well she should.

It was a nice pen, a pole pen. Dad had cut the poles to length from dead young trees, which the older and bigger trees had robbed the sunlight from. These he attached to trees and post to make a beautiful, for horse people, corrals and for cow people, pens. At the south end he built a nice shelter with a manger and there ensconced the cow. She was to calve soon, and the approving nod from this matronly cow indicated that Dad's efforts in her behalf were appreciated.

Now in the aforesaid description can there be detected any hint that there would be anything other than a beautiful addition to our farm to render it worthy of a Burl and Ives treatment? That there would be anything but peace and harmony and maybe a little tranquility enjoyed after dinner? We didn't think so, either. Well, maybe a fleeting whiff of apprehension.

You see, along with her charming bovine endowments she was also outfitted with some very beautifully shaped horns. Nice horns that sprouted from her head, and grew out a few inches. They then made a sweeping arc back in towards each other. They never met. Cow horns seldom do. I don't even know if the left horn ever knew what the right was doing. No, they were separated by a gap about the width of a baby's behind, beautiful to look at all shiny white with sharp black tips.

Few farmers have horned cattle anymore. Too many had their ribs tickled with these natural like daggers either fatally or nearly so. And this is not counting the injuries that the cows inflicted on each other. Well the apprehension was fleeting as I say, so we went about our merry way, feeding and watering June. Yep, that was her name. She came with it. It was free so we used it. As I was saying before her name got in the way, we watered and fed and cleaned up after her as we awaited the expected. I probably shouldn't say I quite so freely, as I was only 3 or 4 at the time and didn't really do more than get in the way. I thought it was the least I could. I got better, though, as time went on. Soon the least I could do was the most I could do.

Now we better get Cecilia into the story because this is about her and June in March.

Sometime in March when spring was just showing in the changing of the clouds and there was a little more warmth to the sun; and the first hint of the change in the voices of the birds were heard, but before you could really say spring, sprung. That's when Marisa sprang into the house to announce that June had indeed brought forth her progeny. And what a nice surprise it was. She had brought forth twins, two little black calves. They were cuter than bugs' ears and just as hard to see at night. Well we, of course, had to run out and see this little miracle and we did.

Not only then but for many days after.

On one particular morning Jeremy, me and Cecilia followed Dad out to the woods to watch him feed June and clean the pen. Leo worked alongside him; Jeremy, Cecilia and I leaned on the second rail of the fence and peered over so we could survey the whole scene in the pen.

Jeremy and I don't know when Cecilia left our side, but at some point she did.

The next happenings were like a blur. Dad had turned his back to throw a clutch of hay into the manger. June was near him waiting for it. Suddenly and without warning she swung rapidly around, lowered her head and charged. In a quick few steps she was upon Cecilia. She hooked Cecilia with her head and flung her into a heap of straw manure and snow. In a blur Dad was flying across the pen. Quick as a whip he grabbed June by one horn and smacked her rump with the other, all in a smooth motion, snapping June around. He scooped Cecilia up into his arms just as June was ready to give her another heave-ho and trundled her out of the pen.

Now to have a fling with a mad cow head that sprouts beautiful, but deadly, horns is mighty dangerous; none of this escaped us as we watched June charge and fling Cecilia. Nor did it escape Dad's thoughts as he raced Cecilia to the house with all of us in pursuit. You see, seldom does a cow charge straight on to an opponent that they wish to turn aside. They charge and then hook their opponent with their horn with a sideways thrust of their head, often inflicting a terrible wound. Had she followed this instinctual inclination this time, Cecilia would have been seriously, if not fatally, hurt. As it were, she fit perfectly between the right and left horn, her bottom sat squarely between June's eyes and as June lifted her head to buck her out of the way, Cecilia was catapulted in a beautiful arc into the soft pile of manure and straw. How in the world Dad was able to cover the ground of that corral in such a flash, to turn June away by that horn, and scoop up Cecilia before June could really have hurt her the second time was truly amazing. We marvel to this day.

Now as to why June did this was perfectly natural. Her calves were not over by her as Dad was feeding. They had lingered over by the fence opposite to her, and this is where Cecilia had crawled through the rails into the pen. June saw Cecilia all bundled up in her winter clothes as a threat to her calves and charged her. A farmer must know the disposition of his cows when they calve because some don't mind a bit if you handle their calves, but others, who are otherwise perfectly docile become deadly when their calves are perceived to be in danger.

When the calves were old enough to be on their own, we sent June on. From then on we either bought cows that were polled (bred in such a way that they don't grow horns) or we de-horned the ones that grew them. God sent a gentle message that day, and we heeded it. We still had Cecilia, these shorn cows do look a bit bald but they seem content not to be shunned, just shorn.

DON'T SHOOT! SORT OF

I didn't know what a mugwump was then. I hadn't met any. Not so's I'd know anyways. Nothing just came up to me and said. "Hello, I am a mugwump." So I have remained mugwumpless to this day. I have met some wigwams, though. Well not actually met one, just read a lot about them in the cowboy and Indian books that Jeremy and I and the others read. The Indians lived in and about them, and nobody seemed to get hurt. Maybe it's different if the wam doesn't have a wig I guess, but I don't know. Well, we had a wam in the family for about three years. You see, when Damien was about 2, and started talking, for some strange reason, he called Tristan waum. How he got this name for Tristan, not one of us could figure. Could be that Tristan's huge brown eyes made him look like a wombat, but how Damien at that age could discern that was a mystery. Although come to think of it, there is a lot of flyover country when a stork is making a delivery, and we might remember that Damien's stork had quite a load and when laboring stertorously over Madagascar. It probably lost a lot of altitude from exhaustion and Damien got a look-see at a wombat in its natural habitat. Be that as it may, Tristan was Waum. And so that's the puzzle, just how do things get such strange names? Perhaps it's just to add a little spice to tales?

Dear reader, you are probably wondering what this has to do with the price of tea in China, being that it is so close to Madagascar and all, but it doesn't. Not really. It's just my short way of getting to my story about how I was shot in the ear by a Rosehip. Yes a Rosehip. Hey, why roses have hips is about as strange as mugwumps, wigwams, bald wams or brother waums. But I did catch one in the ear and this is how it happened.

"You kids get back," Leo turned and yelled and whispered at the same time. He was trying not to scare any game away as he and Andy were trying to hunt with their slingshots. "You guys go back home or stay waaayy back," he hissed through clenched teeth.

"What!?" Jeremy and I chorused together a half whisper and holler.

"Get back now!" Leo again said, expostulating wildly with his arms for emphasis. Now, that motion seemed to have a little more intensity to it and Jeremy and I both pondered what the consequences might be if we didn't go back. Not much pondering though, we kept on walking so as to keep him and Andy in sight. It was a little scary out there in the woods.

What was going on here was that the two great white hunters, Leo and Andy, were being followed by two little anxious boy hunter wannabes. And when a little boy wants to be something, he doesn't just 'go back' early. Leo and Andy had left home, turned up the road to the mailbox, turned left up a little country lane. They then veered off on a veritable wagon road, which lead through a bull pine forest to a green meadow a mile farther on. We were all a lot younger then, about 6 and 7, and it seemed like a mile from home. I can say 'we' because Jeremy and I didn't want to be left behind so we followed a couple of hundred feet behind Leo and Andy, just enough to keep them in sight as they appeared and disappeared around curves in the forest and brush. Leo and Andy could have lost us easily, but they were also trying to hunt and that slowed them down. They were getting a bit frustrated at having these little boys dogging their tails, but we were getting a ways from home; so if Leo and Andy tried to leave us now, they would be in big trouble if we could not find our own way back home.

"You boys go home now." Leo again said, disjointing

his whole body while contorting it and gesticulating wildly in an attempt to scare us good. Jeremy and I, not scaring, moved forward a little bit more. Now during this little follow and leading, Leo and Andy had left the wagon road, and were up on a ridge about 70 yards up and to our left and in front about 30 yards. We were down in a small meadow and they were up by the tree line. This frustration of having two little brothers trailing him on a hunting trip just finally got too much for him, and Leo had had enough. In a fit of desperation he looked for something that could be flung at us that would stop us. Put a little scare in us and hope we would hightail it for home. Well he had the sling to do the fling, but he didn't have what needed to be flung; so he grabbed what was nearest and he slung it with his sling.

What he slung was a rose hip. There was a plethora of them, as there were wild rose bushes growing abundantly all around our place. We were on the border of Half Moon prairie and Wild Rose prairie. The bush he reached into was loaded with rose hips. Now a rose hip is a berry that forms after the flower leaves. It's the seedpod of the bush. It's a nice round shiny red, hard berry. They're not very heavy, but the perfect size for a slingshot pouch. It was this that Leo plucked from the bush and fingered into his slingshot pouch.

Why roses needed hips I don't know. There are climbing roses, there are creeping roses and there are roses with runners, so I guess with all that ambulating they need hips like any others who go wandering about.

Anyway, Leo flung this hip at us intending by this show of force that he meant business. He had no intention of hitting us. His anger did not lead him to desire bodily harm. It was meant only to fly by as a warning. Well, when he let this projectile loose, it headed our way with a zing. We could see it coming. Leo and Andy could see it going. Everything was developing fine. Its trajectory was about 25 degrees south by southwest and should zing by us about 3 feet to the south. But this rose hip was not content to be slung. It began to slew. Whereas it was headed southerly, it began to slew to the northeast. Then the unthinkable happened. It curved a beautiful arc and my eyes grew bigger as it curved toward me. Leo and Andy were frozen in horror as the berry continued to slew down on a course, southeast and headed for Jeremy and me. It seemed as if it sped up as it veered towards us and zap! Before I had time to move, the berry caught me on the ear. Wham! It seemed to have about torn my ear off. I was looking straight at it as it came. Just 1 inch to the left and it would have gotten my eye. One tic to the right and it would have missed entirely and there would be no story. As it were it caught my ear.

Well, I let out a howl of protest. Leo and Andy stood transfixed. Could such an innocent shot have turned to such disaster? Had Nathaniel been hit in the eye? Was I to be blind forever? Unthinkable! Wow! If Dad knew that a slingshot had been shot at anyone, not only would it have been taken away, the coyotes that my howl had aroused from their afternoon nap would have smelt the scent of tanned leather as the hips of Leo and Andy turned from rose to red with Dad's lesson imprinted on them.

These were thoughts that scrambled around in Leo's mind as he stood. Then like any God-fearing child raised in the presence of the Lord, a biblical plan of action began to form. With this he leapt into action. Andy followed. They tore down the hill like their pants were on fire. Over bushes and boulders they leapt, under branches and around logs they ran. If there was a river, he would have swum it. Fast. An idea was forming in Leo's fertile mind. Hadn't he heard in the Bible that the Lord had said that if one has a quarrel with his brother that it was better to wrangle a settlement before his brother brought him to the judge? Yes he did. Chapter and verse escaped him in the frenzy of the moment, but the wisdom was unmistakable. Certainly at 13, he could placate a brother of 6. If his eye was not actually out there was hope. And placate he set about doing just as soon as he and Andy slid to a stop before Jeremy and me and could see that my eyes were doing what they did best, just where they were supposed to be. But I was crying. The sting of the assault had already began to subside by the time they got there, but I had worked up a good howl and I thought that it was worth quite a lot of placating before such a beautiful thing was to be given up.

When Leo could see that it wasn't my eye about four years were added back to his life. Now that the consequences to my person were seen to be minimal, my ear wasn't even bleeding, he could see that his greatest task was to mollify my feelings. Promises and bribes began to flow effusively from his mouth as he sought to mollify me from this mis-adventure and elicit the promise that I would not tell Dad.

It was not a plot to deceive, no real harm had been done and the Bible did say to reconcile with ones brother before being taken before the judge. I don't remember any of the actual inducements. I don't think I needed any. To tell on Leo would not have seemed right anyway and his apologies were plenty sufficient. They were our introduction into the wonders of nature, hunting, fishing, and all that; the fact that we could follow them was enough for me.

It didn't quite end there. Our little secret was almost set free when my hair was scrubbed of all the debris it had collected in it out in the woods. As Mom lathered my head and scrubbed behind my ears she noticed that my ear was noticeably swollen and red. But there wasn't any cut, though. She asked what I did to it. I didn't lie. I don't remember what I said, but she quickly lost interest since there was no sign of my brains actually leaking out.

In Rose's view there was not enough in there to rise to the level of the ear to have fear of that, but that view although common was simply an inability to recognize genius. I hear Einstein had a similar problem when young; it's just taking a little more time for me to arrive at that distinction, given the general sinking of the IQ in the general population as measured by myself. Now, it was Mom's view that there was precious little in there to begin with. A leak may very well have been catastrophic. Any other injuries paled in comparison and were soon forgotten. With the draining of the bathwater, the affair of the rose hip was relegated to the halls of memory only to come out again when not getting in the way of more adventures.

Well, mugwumps, wigs, Waums and rose hips notwithstanding, I continued to follow Leo and Jeremy. You have to keep reading if you want to come too.

DADS BEES AND ME AND MRS. HICKELGRUBER

Of the many adventures I had with Dad, this one saunters forth from my memory as one of the finest. This is on account of Mrs. Hickelgruber. A way up north of our farm, 60 miles or so the way the crow flies, lived this very old lady. She was the grandmother of a fellow who Dad knew at work. She lived in a very small, very old little house tucked into an overgrown orchard and garden. Its dilapidated structure is now mostly collapsed and the trees and vines have buried it almost into oblivion. It was already about to that state when Dad was requisitioned to see if we could get a honeybee hive out of its walls.

In those days most of the old houses had no insulation between the studs of the walls and this little cottage was no exception. The long hollow space between two studs was ideal for honeybees to construct their labyrinth of honeycombs. Dad and I were able to ascertain that measuring from the entrance hole of the hive (a missing knothole in the outside planking of the wall) to the bottom of the honeycombs (we could hear them buzzing with our ear to the wall) within was about 4 feet tall. It was certainly quite a massive hive.

Now the request was that we would remove the nest alive, do no damage to the house, and do nothing to scare the old lady. We set about the planning, as this was a daunting request, but the challenge of it was exciting. I say we. Daddy was really the brains and the brawn. I was about 12 and the manner in which Dad talked to me of it was as if I were an equal partner, and I proffered my suggestions and listened to all of his proposals with all the circumspection I could muster.

The first proposition we tried was to drill a hole in the wall where we thought the end of the hive was. Then we could smok'em out of the top hole, by pouring the smoke into the bottom hole. The smoke travelling up the inside of the wall through the honeycombs labyrinth would hopefully have them rushing out of the top hole, with the result being that the scout bees that are sent out to find a home would find the empty beehive we had all set up just a few yards away. We even put some frames of honeycombs into the new hive to entice them into it. This did not work.

Some of you are wondering where we got the smoke. Well bee men have these little cans with a chimney on them and a bellows attached. You put some burning wood chips in, and pump the bellows and there you have ready-made canned smoke.

This little chimney we would apply to the small hole at the bottom of the wall and start puffing. We quickly saw that the amount of smoke necessary to cause an evacuation would have smoked out Mrs. Hickelgruber also and it was easy to see that a stout German lady from the old country smoked out of her house, wielding an even more stout corn husk broom could have more dire consequences to our persons than even irate stings from the bees. We quickly abandoned that idea for our next.

Well the next idea did not involve smoke, but it did light a fire in our trousers. We thought that if we made their entryway in and out of the hive into a one way out passage we might be able to capture such a great number of them that by attrition they would eventually all quit the house.

So Dad in his meticulous way made a bee cage. The idea was that as the worker bees left the hive to gather nectar we could have them fly into the cage. To keep them from returning back into the hive from the cage we used a little bee trapdoor. It was a little wooden box that the bees would have to enter in on their way out of the house and come out the other side into the cage. It was a one way bug box, with a little tunnel they could only go one way through. Once the bees left they couldn't return. The cage was made out of stiff wire, a cylinder about two feet in diameter and three feet long. We eventually mounted this to the side of the house and hoped to capture the bees in that way.

Now, there had been two obstacles to getting this mounted. One was the obligatory visit to Mrs. Hickelgruber before starting work, and the other, angry bees.

The first was a great pleasure although it required some manly endurance. With her quaint German ways, her fussiness to afford our visit with the greatest of pleasure, her obvious delight in entertaining us, to communicate without the ability to understand each other, all made it a wonderful time. So it wasn't that we didn't want to visit with her. It just involved some pain and discomfort.

You see, she was as we saw an elderly German lady about 85 years old. She lived alone, spoke very broken English. She had come over from Germany itself and her English probably got dropped or something on the ship on the way over and got broke. Anyways she had kept her old German ways. She was always in an old peasant dress, with an apron, a bandanna tied in her hair, very thick soled large shoes and thick stockings. Short, stocky and strong she was and we were charmed by her.

Her tiny house was in disrepair though. Old tarpaper shingles made to look like red brick were falling and hanging off the sides of the house, leaving the planks exposed to the elements. The old tin roof, patched and rusting with the seasons loyally shook off the inclemency of the weather. Vines of various kinds crawled out from the old flower beds that no longer kept them contained, found their way out and climbed about on the old house.

Although Mother Goose still lingered about to help mothers tuck their youngsters into bed at night, the other geese had all flown south and we were well into summer time by the time we were attempting this bee thing. Ninety degree weather was there to greet our day as often as not, as it was on this day.

As usual, we arrived and walked up to the front door and knocked. A shuffle could be heard as Mrs. Hickelgruber moved to the door and let us in. We walked into the almost dark interior, as she only had a feeble light streaming in over her little table that she had pushed up against the kitchen wall under a small murky window. We settled ourselves into our places and were greeted with an almost unbearable heat. She would have made a pot of coffee and some cakes or cookies and the heat of the cook stove added to the summer heat. She would be dressed in her thick German clothing. We would be in thicker than usual for summer clothing, to ward off the stings. Dad was in his big grey striped overalls and me in jeans and flannel shirt.

The first time was the worst as we had to acclimatize to our new surroundings. We got better at it over subsequent visits but they all went virtually the same. As she set out cups for coffee she would assume that I wanted some. I would look across to Dad to see if it were okay. He would nod yes, which was unusual but this was an unusual experience. You see, we weren't allowed to drink coffee at that age. It was said to stunt our growth. The strongest coffee I had ever had was the last drop Dad would sometimes let us have which was mostly sugar that had settled to the bottom of his cup.

The coffee came out of her pot as black as midnight and scalding hot. We poured pounds of sugar in and quarts of milk but to no avail. It remained hot and bitter and virtually undrinkable. Her obvious hospitality, though, required of us to manfully buck up and swig it down. So that we did. My tender mouth was no match for it I am afraid and it remained scalded for days. Dad fared better but he would relate sometime later that he labored under the strain as well.

Oh! But the stifling heat. Could it have been less than 110 degrees? There would be Dad, all politeness and attention carrying on a conversation that even he was mostly at a loss as to what was said. I would see him, sweat pouring from his face drinking hot coffee and eating cake, with me languishing as if to faint at any moment and trying to look causal.

Now as near as I could tell the conversation that commenced with our arrival went something like this.

"Magst du das Wetter, ja?"

We nodded our approval enthusiastically taking the clue from her inflection at the end of her question that something nice was inferred.

As she turned to the stove and began to rustle the cakes on the top,

"Möchten Sie eine Tasse Kaffee?

Again it seemed a question that inferred an affirmative response so we again nodded smilingly. She began to pour thick black coffee for three so we assumed we answered that right.

"Milch und Zucker auch?" Als ich in Deutschland als ein kleines Mädchen war als mein Vater verwendet Dicke gelbe Sahne von der Milch oben kann und am Sonntag zwei Klumpen des Zuckers. Manchmal ließ er uns kleinen nehmen Sie einen Schluck aus seiner Tasse. Ich habe nur Kondensmilch nun aber möglicherweise möchten Sie einige. Ja?

Since she was already bringing the milk and sugar after pouring the coffee we indicated by gesture that we indeed wanted some and by her smiles and action believed we got that right. But as to the other it was guess work and Dad guessed.

"Oh yes it was a beautiful drive up. The flowers are still blooming along the creek and the farmers are beginning to cut the hay." This response seemed to please her very much.

"Als Sie so viele Kuchen haben nach Belieben, ich habe erst heute Morgen gebacken und sie sind immer noch heiß."

She rounded up some small plates and placed some cake slices thereon. While eating, Dad said.

"We are going to mount a cage to trap the bees in today; you may hear some pounding on the wall."

At the same time he made hammering motions with his hand in the direction of the house where we would be working.

"Als Sie so viele Kuchen haben nach Belieben, ich habe erst heute Morgen gebacken und sie sind immer noch heiß." She stated.

Once again by the inflection of her comment we sensed an affirmative shake of the head was called for so we bobbed accordingly.

Now did you understand that? Well, neither did I. I nodded heartily and feelingly though and Dad soldiered on in this manner of conversation with Mrs. Hickelgruber through his scalding coffee and pastry. After what seem like an infernally long time we would graciously bow out and stagger into the relative coolness of the hot summer day. There to again tackle the bee problem.

So now that the first, although pleasant, obstacle to mounting the cage was overcome, we launched into our task. Dad climbed the ladder with the cage on his shoulder, with hammer hanging from his overalls hammer loop and nails in his mouth, and I held onto the bottom of the ladder to steady it while Dad maneuvered around trying to hold up the cage and attach it the house at the same time. He had left three mounting tabs of wood protruding from the end and front side of the cage through which he could pound nails thus attaching it to the house.

He had just started hammering the first nail in with loud vigorous strokes, when predictably I suppose, the bees, after being smoked, pounded and prodded lost patience and turned their righteous indignation to wrath and attack. Out of the entrance hole the hive disgorged a whole company of guard bees to defend their fort. The cage was not mounted well enough yet to seal the bees in. And they were out. They were after us. I left Dad swaying on the ladder as I headed for the thicket of the overgrown orchard. I dove into the brambles trying to evade this army of honeybees that were now madder than hornets. Now that I just said that, they really were insulted, as they felt they could muster as much wrath as a respectable honeybee as any hornet and took umbrage at having to borrow the hornet's reputation to augment their own.

So now I was really in trouble and sought safety from their angry stings. I plunged into the thicket, flailing about, zigzagging as fast as I could, losing one bee and another in the confusion of the brambles. Still a few dogged me. Scratched and bleeding already, one zapped me on the back, piercing through my shirt and I let out a yelp. I swatted him with my hand and looked wild eyed for more as my back smarted from the sting. All was quiet. I had lost them. I was unsure whether or not I had scratched my eyes clean out in all the brambles, so, taking no chances I mimicked a nursery rhyme I remembered that Mother Goose offered in a case like mine.

There was a man in our town,
And he was wondrous wise,
He jumped into a bramble bush,
And scratched out both his eyes;
But when he saw his eyes were out,
With all his might and main,
He jumped into another bush,
And scratched 'em in again.

So I leapt back into the bush to scratch my eyes back in. It didn't work. I was worse off than before. I learned the brutal and hard truth that you just can't believe everything that you read. Skin and clothes in tatters I ran around the house to find Dad still busily at work tacking the cage up. His coveralls were thick enough to ward off the stings. He nearly fell off the ladder, laughing at my panicked flight when he saw my return. Nor could I when I regained my composure keep from joining him. It was rather comical. Darn bees!

Well we never did get those bees out of there. The cage idea didn't work. Only a few hundred bees came through the trap. The rest started finding holes that led inside Mrs. Hickelgruber house. That wouldn't do at all. She wanted her honey in a jar. Sticky fingers was about the worst thing to happen getting your honey that way but try and uncork a honeybee and pour out his honey was mighty risky even when he was in the best of humor. A stinging rebuke was likely. She didn't want them in the house.

We did our level best though to get them out but we couldn't. We were of the same mind as her that to destroy a honeybee hive just didn't seem right and she suffered them to stay.

Yes I still remember us cruising up the highway turning on the byways, windows, rolled down, arm on the window sill, talking with Dad, feeling all grownup as we headed up north to Mrs. Hickelgruber's. Better grab an empty seat if you want a ride to the next adventure.

SNOW

There was 90 feet of very steep broad hillside. That was one of the features the old mine provided for us to use. There was 90 feet with 2 feet of thick snow blanketing it. It was a tobogganer's paradise. But whence were the toboggans? Our finances were just a tad too thin to be able to purchase these beautifully fashioned works made by able craftsman's hands out of hickory, oak or some such beautiful hardwood; so something else was required.

The solution came by accident. Sticking out of the dirt where it was partially buried in mine tailings was the metal of an old car hood. With some digging and pulling Leo and Andy had unearthed a huge car hood, and part of a chrome ornament still graced the center of it. It was so heavy, made of such thick-gauged steel, it seemed as if the car manufacturer simply took the plate armor off an old WWII tank and bent it into shape to cover the powerful motor of some American-made touring car. This discovery took place during the summer and except for the occasional rocks that were bounced off it in passing it sat neglected. But when the snow beckoned to be slid on, Leo remembered this junk and turned it into a jewel. Flip it onto its top and there we had a Detroit-built toboggan.

If cars weighed about 6 tons then, and this was a 1950s vintage, then this hood alone took about a ton of it. The front curved way up and back just like a toboggan. It was way wider though, almost as long as it was wide. The sides curved up just slightly. The back was curved to accommodate the rounded windshield when it was on the car. Consequently when the sides met the rear of the car hood it left two large pieces of metal protruding from the rear corners almost like two short bullhorns of steel. This surely was the answer to a prayer.

I was only about 8 at the time so I was not part of the maiden voyage of this ship of the frozen slanted sea. No, that was left to Louisa, Elizabeth, Leo, Marisa and Andy. First, we had to get it up the hill. Well, it was just too hard to muscle it up the steep part where it would come down, so it was dragged around the flank of the hill and around to the brink where it would be shoved off. There, these five kids would pile on, all facing the front. Yes, the hood was that big, it could fit them all. With a heave ho and shout they leaned forward and shot down the hill. With screams of half terror and half delight the car hood raced down. Not content with just looking forward as forced to do when on the car, it flaunted its freedom and let loose. It bucked, spun, and twirled, bounced high as it threw rooster tails of snow in every direction and headed down the hill in reckless abandon. The kids held on for dear life as this mad steel behemoth tried to throw them off its back. When it reached the bottom it shot across the flat so fast that it flattened the kids. The angle was so sharp from the steepness of the hill to the plane of the bottom that it whiplashed the rider so as to flatten him to the floor. Now prone they headed for the woods. That had not been bargained for. What now? Throw themselves unceremoniously into the snowdrifts and hope for the best or ride the ship out. Fortunately when they thought it best to throw themselves off, the beast was caught in the deep snow, and stopped. Laughing and talking they knocked the snow off each other, grabbed the homemade toboggan and started pulling it for another ride.

It took a good two months before I acquiesced to try a ride. All the kids down to Jeremy had braved this monster but me. One day I labored along with Leo and Andy, Jake and Jeremy as we tugged our 1-ton toy up the flank of the hill. I had a nervous stomach and thought of a million excuses why this ride was not to my advantage. None worked. The one millionth and one almost did. It almost convinced me to just agree that I was a coward and leave it at that but with the assurances and encouragements fired at me from my older brothers I sent that excuse packing. A small pack, though, as if he didn't intend to be gone for long, hoping I might summon him back. So he didn't leave in a hurry, sort of just slunk away and I looked at him wistfully a few last times as we piled onto the sled.

But that was an excuse I was glad to part with once I made up my mind; so there I was perched on the edge, ready to plunge down. With a shout we shoved off. It was a lot worse than I thought. My right hand clutched the cold hard steel of the side, my left arm clutched in desperation around Andy. As we careened down, snow flew in clouds and filled my nose, mouth and eyes. The car hood spun around and nearly left my head behind. I clutched so hard to that steel it seem to buckle in my grip. Andy surely was no anchor. He was bopped up and down like a jumping bean as the hood bucked around like a confused bronco. Blue sky, swirling snow, trees, winter hats and clothing all got mixed as my eyes sought refuge in that rapidly revolving world. Half hollering, half laughing, and half hoping (by this time I didn't have half a chance at deciphering correctly) I would make it to the end, we flew down, and then with a wham we were flattened on our backs as it hit the bottom and slid out onto the straight.

I staggered up onto my feet, wobbly and a bit disoriented, as I tried to see out of my snow-packed eyes. Snow was packed around my arm above my mittens threatening to freeze my arm off right then and there. Andy and Leo began to beat the snow off of both of themselves and us. They were all full of fun and asked me how I liked it. I shook my head in approval as my frozen lips couldn't quite form intelligible sounds yet. My millionth and one excuse sort of sidled up to see if I would need him if asked if I wanted to go for another ride, but I was saved from his temptations by Mom's call that it was suppertime.

Our friendly association with this monster came to an end one day as one of the kids flew off and was almost clobbered by one of the steel horns as it joyously flung children in every direction. Leo realized that if in fact this hood actually flipped or swung and hit one of us, the result could be catastrophic. It was a goal of Moms and Dads to shuttle us through life with all the limbs we came with at birth and Leo thought it best to encourage this idea. The behemoth was retired.

But...he (that's the car hood not Leo) had children. Oh yes! Progeny. It didn't take Andy and Jeremy's resourcefulness very long to get us back to serious snow sailing. They found scraps of galvanized sheet metal. Not wimpy little thin gauge sheet metal used for air ducts or housetops, but thick heavy gouge sheet metal used for sluice chutes in mining containers or some such requiring strength and endurance. These scraps measured about two feet by four feet, but were all mangled up by the huge bulldozers as they pushed rocks and debris around the mining sight, abandoned with only parts peeking from the ground.

Andy and Jeremy hauled these pieces home and set to work. First task was to get the wrinkled bent up mess flat. Nothing worked to de-bend the bends, but Dad's 4- pound sledgehammer. Dad had this 3-inch thick piece of steel about 18 inches square that he used as sort of an anvil. Setting their mangled piece of metal on this block, they began to pound it with the sledgehammer. Even then little progress was made. The metal was so thick that it barely bent as it was struck. The sledge mostly bounced off when it struck. Since we didn't know which direction it would bounce, this required all of us to stand way back as the boys pounded. Slowly, but surely, they commandeered this reluctant metal back to flatness. Relative flatness, that is. Having been so mangled it left stretch lines all over as it was forced back into shape and so it gave the metal an almost marbled surface. But for boys bent on being on the hills, it would do. They grabbed the front edge of the tin and bent it back towards them into a perfect toboggan front. Since it was a bit springy, they got a piece of baling wire to hold it in place. This was logical, three-quarters of machinery and buildings on small farms of those days were held together with baling wire and this needed holding.

Now onto the hills we went. They tied a piece of baling twine to the front and towed their creations up the hill. Now for the test run. A test run in this context does not mean that you try something first in a safe and sterile environment to see if it going to work before applying it to real-life situations. Test runs simply meant it was the first time you did it. If you lived through the experiment, it worked and was good to go. If not, you were expendable in the name of exhilarating adventures and were a good example to the remaining 14 siblings of what not to do.

Well, they jockeyed their sheet metal toboggans into position and shoved off. They really flew down that hill. Some of the swells and vales of the snow track causing them to go airborne as they raced down the hill. What a hit! What engineering! We all clamored for a turn. One after another we rode those sheets of steel down the fast track of frozen snow. Many times hurtling off the beaten track into the thick powdery snow drifts, nearly buried, and then untangling arms, legs and winter clothing as we got back up. Sometimes squishing two even three kids on at the same time and hurtling down until the kid train fell apart in a flurry of clothes, snow, and tumbling kids. We had a blast. It never occurred to us at the time that all that speeding and twisting and turning and wipeouts, that that sheet metal could have virtually decapitated us with its thin edges: or at least had left serious slashes and gashes.

We used those toboggans for years. They were even pressed into service in other ways also. For sometimes for two or three months at a time we would be snowed in. Not completely in. But in as far as driving in or out was concerned. Then, we'd have to cart all our groceries, press-to-logs, (heavy pressed sawdust logs to augment our fire wood supply) and water jugs, (glass gallon jugs we filled with water from town when our well went dry) down to the house by hand. That was the work for us boys and the older girls and of course Dad when he wasn't at work. Mom had her work cut out carrying tykes and towing toddlers. It was a quarter of a mile from the county road at the mailbox where we could park down our road to the house. In snowstorms, drifts or rain and slush we trekked that road countless times up and down over the years. Those toboggans came in useful to pile with goods and pull supplies down to the house. But the best part was when they carried us down the hill at breakneck speeds, us clinging on for dear life.

Yes, the big steel car hood begot two little steel toboggans and his family and ours enjoyed many happy hours together.

Now, there was an alternative to using toboggans at all. When the toboggans would have gone down the hill often enough in the same track, it would leave a hard packed surface. This would reduce the friction and faster speeds were realized the more times we went down. At some point it would pack enough we could just go down on our stomach or back just wearing our winter clothes. When going down you had to really tighten your coat about your throat or tighten up your sweatshirt hood to keep the snow from scooping into your jacket and down your neck. It was the best to go down on your back, headfirst.

Usually the many trips down the hill formed the track into a trench somewhat, much like the luge tracks in the Olympic Games. This track we lowered ourselves into, on our backs, and shoved off. Down the hill we would fly, backwards and headfirst, bumping up and down on little swells and valleys of the track, sometimes so hard it would almost knock the breathe out of us. Had to keep your mouth clamped shut as not to bite your tongue and hoped nothing bad had wandered into the track on your way down. You couldn't see and even if you could, you weren't stopping. Even the occasional bear had to ponder if it were really worth trying to cross our track what with a human torpedo likely to take its feet out from under them. We never saw any, so they must have been figured it wasn't safe to cross our tracks.

Well, one day when we had really fast luge track developed, a neighbor boy who had just moved in about a mile away, came out to join us. He was a good many years older, I think he was down trying to get Elizabeth's attentions, and decided to wander up into the mine where we were sliding and say hi. So far so good. He watched the way some of us flew down the hill on our backs, some screaming, some clenching their teeth and all having a wild ride. He thought this looked like a lot of fun and asked if we minded if he took a turn. We answered enthusiastically that "no we didn't mind." He looked kind of fancy in that ski jacket and we thought it might be kind of fun to see if anything interesting would happen.

So he flipped the hood of the ski jacket up over head

and tied the string. We told him to just sit down and lean back and away you'll go. Well that fancy jacket was nice and long so he was able to sit on it too and so he just sat down and immediately started to slide so we yelled "lay, down, lay down," and he did and the next thing he did was shoot out of there like bull out of the chute at the county fair. That ski jacket was made out of nylon or some such thing, and was slicker than wet glass. It offered virtually no resistance to the already slick snow and wow did he fly. At each little swell of the track he was launched into the air only to have gravity and speed to conspire and slam him back onto the ground. His head was whiplashed up and down like a bobber on a fishing line and his breath was pounded out of his lungs with each bounce as he weaved and bobbed, flew and whammed down the hill.

We watched in stunned amazement as he sped down the hill. As he reached the bottom of the track and met the flat ground, he shot along the flat and far outdistanced the end where we usually stopped. An explosion of snow engulfed him as he disappeared for a moment. When we could see him he lay there for a moment as if dead. Than with a few groans he began to move and then hoisted himself to his feet. He stood there completely blinded. Snow so packed between his glasses and his eyes that they looked like goggles. His breath came in great gasps and he tried to refill with what had been pounded out of him in his wild descent. We slid down to him as fast as we could to make sure he was okay, and when assured he would survive we began to scheme of how we could get a ski jacket. That was the wildest, fastest, and funniest ride, we'd ever seen and we were determined to imitate it. He, however was so beat up he didn't have the judgment left to notice if he had fun. With all his teenage bravado and dignity beaten out of him, he hauled his sore and sorry carcass off to home.

How we got hold of an old blue ski jacket I don't remember, but I sure do remember the thrill of leaving the ground and than being slammed back down so hard your breath was cleaned knocked out of you. Your tailbone hammered so hard you thought it was nailed permanently to your hips. It made walking a humorous affair but as long as you could manage to get yourself to the top of the hill, it worked well enough. Forget about the pain, it was about the speed that made it all worthwhile.

Smoking Carp, Eating Crow

Just how do you smoke carp? I had no experience smoking. I had seen some of the kids at school sneaking a cigarette. But that was tobacco I think. This was the 1970s and I heard that you could smoke cannabis. Some kind of large mammal from Africa I should think, probably a lot like a camel. I'd seen boxes with those on it. So maybe you could smoke a carp. But how you'd get this big ugly fish into a wrapper? I didn't know, possibly a pipe was more suited to this enterprise. If you could fit a pot into a bowl and smoke it maybe you could fit a carp into a pipe.

Well, it was Andy who introduced Jeremy and me to smoking fish. Turned out it was way different than I thought. He found a discarded steel 30-gallon drum, cut one end off and punched a hole in the other. He set it aside. He then dug a small pit in the ground, constructed a wire stand that he could hang fish from, and placed this over the pit. He then lifted the drum and slid it down over the rack of fish, and built a small fire in the pit. The excess smoke poured out the top of the little hole and there Andy could suck all the smoke into his lungs that he liked.

Only to my surprise, he was not interested in smoking these fish at all the way I thought. He didn't even take a good breath of it. No, he was to saturate the fish with this smoke as they hung on the racks smothered by the drum. They didn't seem to mind, couldn't kill them I suppose, and so they absorbed all the second-hand smoke they could. Now these were bony squawfish that we for the longest time thought were brook trout. We'd catch them in the same creek our swimming hole was located, but much farther downstream.

Andy would leave these fish to smoke in their haven for a couple days, just stoking his little fire occasionally to keep it smoldering away. Boy, when he lifted that barrel from over these thoroughly smoked fish and we caught a smell of them, we were believers. Andy passed around morsels of these mongrel fish and we picked the smoked flesh from the bones and ate away. It was delicious. The eating pleasure was somewhat marred, however, by the incredibly tedious work of picking out all the little forked bones that threatened to choke us if we didn't pay attention. None of us were eager to call on St. Blasé and test his intercessory powers. But smoking fish was a great success.

Now, there's more than one-way to skin a cat as the saying goes (never tried, just heard it) and I guess this applied to smoking fish, too.

So armed with this experience Jeremy and I determined to smoke carp. If you read the first volume of these tales you know all the about the capturing carp escapades Jeremy and were involved in. If you haven't, you must stop and buy one now, or maybe two or three, pass them amongst friends so no one misses the fun.

Well, these carp that we shot were 30 to 40 inches long and weighed in at about 30 pounds. They were considered junk fish, bottom eaters, and good for nothing suckers only good but for fertilizer; but we had read that the Europeans had a way of preparing them that would transform them into a delicacy. If Europeans could do it, certainly Americans could.

So we set about getting set up for it. First, we gutted an old steel refrigerator so only the shell remained. And then we cut some sticks to lengths that spanned the inside and there upon hung the massive fish. We started with just two to begin with, to see how it went. We had soaked them the night before in brine made of water, salt, cinnamon, ketchup and other seasonings.

We cut our workload down by not filleting them into slices. Besides, they were so darn greasy you could hardly hold onto them, as they slithered around the cutting board. This should have been our first clue that all was not right, but we soldiered on.

We set our smoker close to an old camper that Leo had parked by a power pole. This had two advantages, one it had electricity and two it had a bed and a floor to sleep on. This combination worked out nicely, as we had a small hotplate plugged in, whereon we placed wood chips that would smolder all night, providing our smoke. This was placed in the bottom of the fridge so the smoke would rise up and envelope the fish. About every hour we had to get up and put on more wood chips to keep the smoldering chip pile from burning out. Now, that wouldn't have been so bad if that was all the night entailed, but Dad asked a favor to be done for him. Our getting up hourly would be just the thing. That was this.

He recently had a new well drilled up in the farthest corner of the property at the end of the east-west fence line. That would be a quarter of a mile from where we snuggled blissfully in our sleeping bags. The well man had said that it was best to run the well water pump continually for 24 hours to make sure the water stayed flowing freely. There was a danger, though, that the new well would run dry and ruin the pump. A dry running pump would overheat if left too long, so he asked if we would run up and check the water coming out of the end of the continuously running hose to make sure that the well hadn't run dry.

This complicated the already unpleasant task of stoking the fire. The alarm would jar us awake, we would furtively get out of our blankets while only in skivvies and with our eyes half closed, sneak out to the smoker and add a few wood chips to the pile on the hotplate. We'd then slink back into our blankets undetected by rodent or reptile and go back to sleep before really having to wake up. But now, we had to get jarred awake, get up drunk with sleep, put some clothes on, albeit cold shoes, shirt, and clammy smoked-filled pants and then blearily stagger to the chips and stoke the fire and then start out for the well.

We had two choices to get there, run all the way and back with our heart pounding and the chance of a good twisted ankle, this, to get back to the bed as quickly as possible; or stumble all the way up and back, staying as sleepy as possible, in the hopes of staying in a dream like stupor until sliding back into bed. The latter seldom was successful. Not with birds exploding from their night beds, and scaring the bejeebers out of us. It's jittery enough having the bejeebers in you, but having them out there consorting with rest of the frightful creatures was too much. Owls screeched, startled cows stampeded and noises from unknown creatures all pierced the night air. All these together and bejeebers, too, set the heart to racing at least nine times faster than a normal panic and set us into the first option with not so much as a howdy-do. And so most often we ran.

We took turns at this, Jeremy and I. Flashlights were deemed a cowardly instrument, invented by city folks and so we braved the night terrors alone, unlit. It's kind of amazing how much starlight can gather in when your eyes are as big as dinner plates and you never dare to blink. Frozen like this they would hardly get shrunk back down to size before the alarms jangled us out of bed again.

So it was with bleary eyes, smoke and sweat-saturated clothes that we rolled forth for the last time and greeted the early morning. It wasn't easy at first, but as the realization pushed itself through our groggy noggins that we were to cut into delicious smoked, European inspired carp, we eagerly got fully dressed, and grabbed our knives in readiness to cut into the delicacy. We opened the smoker door, whereon we were immediately engulfed in billows of smoke. Blinded, coughing and gagging, we waited for the smoke to clear (don't forget the word gag; we are going to need it in a moment).

When we peered into the hazy interior, there hung the great slabs of carp. Or were they? What actually hung there were huge hunks of grayish fish flesh oozing buckets of oil. Could this be the European delicacy? Or perhaps we fought the Revolution for a reason. This was revolting. But might this repulsive exterior hold culinary delight within? Should we plunge our knives into this quivering mass of gray smoked fish with the distinct possibility they would dissolve away in our hands? Should we taste it? Well, what could it hurt, we reasoned. We ate broccoli under duress and lived to tell about it. What could it hurt? Oh, the indiscretion of youth. We didn't even know what the word meant much less knew if we had any use for it, so we plunged in.

Sort of. We managed to unhook one of these fish and carry it into the house and slide it onto the cutting board. Trying to hold onto this slimy mess and hack away a chunk took the wrestling skills of both of us, so after some agile moves and cries of encouragement we hurled at each other, we got it pinned and cut a nice hunk. The hunk sliced in two, gave us the ability to each chuck one into our mouths simultaneously, thereby not given the other the pleasure of seeing one go down in agony. Nope this was a joint effort and we would soldier on together.

So, one, two, three and we threw our heads back and shucked it in. It got in but it didn't get much about. No sir. No longer had it entered and met the taste buds but that it was nearly chucked forth as fast as it went in. (We can use gag here.) It was barely squeezed by the molars before it scrambled for an exit. It tasted just as nature had designed the fish. It was an oily, spongy rubber substance, with a disgusting pungent smoked mud taste, and that is being polite. We spat it to the ground in no time flat and looked at each other in shock. Our taste buds were still trying to recover from their fright when we burst out laughing. It was the only antidote from this poisonous mess we had concocted and we laughed until our bellies ached. Laughing and smacking each other on the back, we headed from the house. We cast a guarded glance at each other once in a while just to make sure there wasn't a delayed poisonous reaction and we didn't go into convulsions or something. No, we had survived. Had to have or I wouldn't be here to tell you about when we ate crow. First, though, we buried the carp. Not a lot of ceremony, just a simple little hasty burial. We didn't need to leave a marker, the worms turned away in disgust and the plants around just up and withered away. So that's enough of our tales and testimony to our carp smoking days.

Now, I don't remember how Jeremy popped a crow. They were sly folks. You couldn't just saunter out and say I want to eat crow today and viola! There's a skinned crow. He got one, though, and we were to make a feast of it. The carp caper had faded a bit and anyhow the eating of crow came from a respectable outdoor magazine from America. We weren't about to be taken in by just any old European claims this time. No sir, these were bona fide American claims.

Now Mom was a bit skeptical about us using the kitchen. She was justified in her apprehensions. After the carp, crawdads, frog legs and such like things that we tried, and were literally retched failures, she wasn't much assured that crow was going to be a crowning achievement. We assured her, though, that we had this one on good authority and nothing could go wrong.

The word feast had to be downgraded from the start. After having plucked this bird, we found that its feathers concealed only a pretty scrawny little carcass. Poking it and turning it about a little plaintively and skeptically we commenced to season it. We popped it into the turkey roaster, set the oven temp and slid it in there to roast. And it did roast. It roasted away mostly. When the beeper went off indicating that time was up, and our imagination having enough time to exaggerate realty by envisioning the likes of a big Thanksgiving turkey, we slid that bird right back out and set it on the counter. Jeremy jerked the lid off, with the rest of the gang looking on and Mom at a safe distance. We all peered in, than we peered again, and a little more. There, now we could see it. It had shriveled its already somewhat measly little self into a pathetic dried out skeleton. The meat clung to the bones so tightly it was stretched like taut ropes running up and down the bone. Our imaginations now deflated, we dug into our repast with as much gusto as we could, to salvage what little we might. Holding the sharp little bones we picked and tore off what stringy meat we could. Well, the crow didn't have a bad taste; he just really didn't have any taste at all. That's right, tasteless. He seemed to have just soaked up all the flavorings we had so generously doused him with and left us with nothing! There was nothing to savor and little to bite. So after a bit, any pretence of making something out of nothing was useless and we just gave up. We threw it all out to see if it could interest the magpies. We couldn't. They loved to harass the crows when they were alive, but just scoffed when they found one cooked. Like us, it lost interest and went to find something more interesting to do. Have you ever tasted muskrat?

Eat Galoshes!

What is it about boys and boots? On the one hand (or should we say on one foot) we couldn't wait to get new boots. We would go into all kinds of histrionics when we received new boots for the winter. But wear boots to school. Horror! What would the other kids think?

Well, that's the way it was with us boys and things would happen like this. In second grade, that formative time when one is reaching full manhood, I received a brand-new pair of boots. Mom pulled them from a sack of goods she had brought from the store and set the box on the table with this admonition. "Do not get holes in these, watch what you're doing, you'll not be getting new ones until you grow out of these." The admonition barely registered on my mind as I dragged the box from the table, and with eager hands opened it to reveal a pair of shiny white plastic boots. These were boots with an actual loop, which you could stretch and hook onto a button to tight'em them up. Plopping myself to the floor I hastily pulled these boots on, the faster to get outside and see just how fast I could run in them. New boots could easily add 20, 30 miles an hour, maybe more on a sunny day, to a dashing boy. Yes siree, you could really fly in new boots. Up from the floor I leapt and headed for the door, before I was collared by Mom. "Get your coat, your hat and mittens on before you go out." What, and lose valuable time? With a lot of squirming on my part and a little exasperation on hers, she wrestled my outdoor clothes on and I was released outdoors. Ah, beautiful, a foot and a half of new snow, untrammeled by old boots of any kind. I sprang from the back porch and began running. Around the first corner of the house I raced, and up along the north side of the house I ran, floundering a bit now as the reality of the deep snow dragged at my legs and feet, pulling at the wings of my fancy, but yet unfazed, I rounded the second corner and was now running past the back of the house. Uh, oh, it was nearly pitch black, no yard light in those days. Deep snow now entwined my feet and I had to labor along. I was beginning to puff. But the thought of slowing down was only a momentary amusing thought. It was one that could be entertained only in the safety of a warm chair and hot cocoa. Neither offered itself out here in the scary dark and cold.

I was in the near total dark and only halfway around the house, as my new boots worked, churning, throwing rooster tails of snow as I plowed my away around the next corner, fear now motivating me. I shot around the third corner, and then my complete faith in my new boots was shaken.. What was that cold feeling gripping my ankles? Can't stop now, but was snow breaking over the ramparts? I sped for the next corner, breathing stertorously. One corner to go and then I'd be at the back door. My boots gripped the snow with all their brand-new strength, as they tried to keep me up as I careened around the last corner. Flagging, stumbling and gasping, I set my eyes on the warm glow of light emanating from the back door window and pushed myself through the snow. Yep, my boots were still with me, but decidedly heavier, a cold band was clamped around my lower leg.

The twin motivators of fear pushing from behind and comfort luring from the front, seemed to pump new life into my new boots, and they sailed me through the deep snow onto the porch. With feverish wrestling I wrested the door open and tumbled into the house. Slamming the door shut to keep the monsters and the cold out, I plopped down to assay how my new boots had performed. Snow had definitely breeched the tops. That was a definite strike against them. On the other hand, I was alive and in the house. They had not loosened and abandoned me out there. The traction of their new soles had kept me upright, and although I had not actually flown, I did sail through the drifts in exhilaration. Digging the snow out that had filled my boots, I decided that after a little drying they would be just fine. New found friends will not be perfect I guess but they stuck with me and sure were fine looking. They passed the test and anyway if they did fail me, I'd just have to take lots of vitamins so I would grow fast and out of them. All my new boots were tested this way; a few laps around the house on their maiden voyages told me how they would perform in the hard adventuring to come.

Only there was one adventure I wished they didn't have to go on and that was school. We had to carry our shoes along with our school books up to the car at the end of the driveway while wearing our boots in the snow. Than at school, when we arrived in the classroom, we had to take them off and change into our shoes. The boots would be placed in the cloak-room along with the coats and hats. They'd rest there until the scramble of excited kids rushed in to retrieve them and put them on for recess. Now the more con-fused the scramble the better it was for the boys. You see Sister (the teacher) tried her best to see that every-one went out into the snow at recess properly attired. But with 35 to 40 students that was a huge task; there were always miscreants who made it through.

And that was the plan, because we hated wearing boots. Why we thought it was cool not to wear them at school, I don't know, as our feet sure froze without them. But frozen feet were preferable to not being cool. The second reason, though, was much more rational. I said much *more* rational. Not completely rational, no wrong doing measures up to that, but it was the freedom of gamboling around in the snow and ice with just a light pair of shoes that was so tempting. It was also here that I was introduced to a foreign language. Sister would say "Now nobody better forget to put your galoshes on." It took the informing of some of my more cosmopolitan classmates to learn that galoshes were boots. Well, call them by a foreign name to see if the mystique would make them more enticing if you like, but we were smart, a boot is still a boot, even when dressed up fancy like with a name like galosh. One can get into trouble with names as we will find out, and we just wanted to get out to the playground without our boots on.

One fine day I managed this feat. I snuck both of my feet out to the playground only shod with a pair of patent leather shoes with a hard slick sole. There was about 3 inches of new, wet, spring snow that blanketed the playground. We all poured out into this snowscape and it quickly turned into 3 inches of icy slush. With gusto I ran, flailing around at first to gain traction, until I got up to a great speed and then slid, and slid, just sailing along, the shoes leaving a wake of slush behind as more slush was sprayed into the air like snow curling off the blade of a snowplow. What freedom, the exhilaration of whipping along freely with no weight of boots. Some of the slush would creep up and over the front of the shoes as I sailed, until finally I came to a stop.

And then, again pushing off and sailing once more, free of school, free of care, and free of boots. In time a little bit of reality would try to seep in, in the form of slush climbing over the sides of the shoe and down inside, tickling my foot with an icy finger. Slowly my shoe became a little limp as it soaked with water and my feet started to grow cold. A little other coldness started to grip my soul as it froze the sole of my shoes. How to explain sopping wet, misshapen shoes to Mom and a pair of nice dry boots when picked up from school? In the midst of pleasure, caution is so quickly thrown to the wind, and the fine breeze that blew on my face made sure it stayed away.

Well the jangling of the recess bell never failed from its duty and it called us in. We all trudged back to the schoolroom. Now the full reality of our misdeeds were revealed. You see, I was not the only boy who had evaded the preternatural gifts that the Nun's possessed. No, here was a good nine or 10 of us caught in this infraction. And how did Sister make sure the culprits could not deny blame with excuses like, *I forgot my boots, the dog chewed them up, or a beggar needed them more than I, and you always said generous giving is sign of great charity?* She had them all lined up on her desk in neat rows in their very dry uniforms. They looked accusingly at us as our very wet shoes squeaked across the floor saying, "We're wet. We're wet." Defense was futile. We slunk to our chairs there to await what retribution might be coming our way.

Well, first we had to take them off, and walk with them each alone, so the whole class could share in our ignominy, and set them on the heat register. There they sat, drying out as the giant fans blew their hot air on them. It didn't take long before the status of semi-hero that we had earned by defying rules and common sense began to change to derision and disgust. Yup, our self- centered rash acts were now drawing the whole class unwittingly into the bad effects of our transgressions. The air was taking on a decidedly pungent odor. Noses began to twitch and expressions of disgust were thrown our way as the realization that this odiferous onslaught came from no other than the drying of a dozen sweat soaked, slush impregnated wet leather. The smell of rotten feet was unmistakable. It worked its way around the classroom, attacking the olfactory nerves of every nose that dared expose itself from being buried in sleeves, scarves or hankies. The sniggering, the "pee you's" made Sister's efforts a bit trying as she tried to direct the attention of the class on the lessons of the day. She was not unawares at the discomfiture our actions had caused in us. We had already slunk to our chairs so slunking had already been used up, we couldn't actually crawl under our desk, so there we sat exposed to the reproachful glares of our innocent classmates. We squirmed under this humiliation and began to sweat as the realization that there would be unpleasant consequences at home also if we arrived at the house carrying dilapidated wet shoes.

I think Sister took pity on our plight. That is why

she made us dry our shoes. She could have made us bring them home and let our transgression tell on itself. But she didn't. She never mentioned our infraction and our misdeeds remained a secret. It's a secret that now only you, me, and Sister know. We never did that again. We bore the self-imposed humiliation of wearing boots to school with manly fortitude, and waited for the next year to try out the flight characteristics of new boots.

I also came away with the new knowledge that boots are galoshes. Sometimes new knowledge can be somewhat frightening.

One day, years later I arrived at a friend's house and was seated for dinner. After saying grace, a steaming bowl of a sort of unrecognizable slurry of food was placed before me. I eyed it quizzedly. I was used to being able to distinguish my meat from the potatoes, the vegetables from the fruit and so on. This mush looked mighty suspicious. I poked furtively at it, making sure nothing unsavory rose from the depths. Next, plucking up courage, I scooped a spoonful and raised it toward my mouth. Just than my host said, in a loud and happy voice, "Boy, have some goulash!" I froze.

They eat boots! I thought, visibly shaken.

My hand stopped mid flight to the mouth. That explained the lumps, the chunks, the stringy pulp. Who had worn these boots? Were they foreign or domestic boots, locally grown and worn or had they traveled far through forest and stream? The thought of eating boots filled me with horror. I knew, having worn many pair from new to dilapidation, what an old experienced boot had trod upon and not entirely divorced itself from. All this is now in the pot? My host could not help but see that my body had gone through a serious jolt and he enquired.

"What's the matter, sick?"

I shook my head no, mumbling, "Not yet."

My eyes arched up questioningly but my arm still frozen in midair.

"You eat galoshes?" my voice quavered.

"Oh yes, we eat goulash all the time, you can practically throw anything into the pot and simmer it for days if you have to, flavors just mix altogether into a delicious soup, you could practically throw your shoes in there and it'd turn out alright," he finished with a flourish, downing a huge steaming spoonful as he closed.

I gulped in dismay. I could hardly believe it. Like those smelly shoes lined up on Sister's radiator in the classroom emitting all those horrible smells? My arm was losing strength. How could I get excused from this table? How could I actually down a spoonful of old boots? I had heard these people were Hungarians but how could a little accent, they say goulash, we say galosh, excuse the eating of boots. Than it struck me, they were Hungarians. That's it Hungary. When hungry it's true, you'll eat about anything. Poor folks, I understood now. A streak of pity smote my heart, and then charity welled up in my breast and I said, "You can come over to our house and eat spaghetti, than you wouldn't have to eat your boots."

Now it was my host's turn to pause, his spoon slowed and he looked first at me with bewilderment and then started laughing.

"Did you say boots?" The mix up had dawned on him.

"Goulash, my lad goulash," he said again. "Not galosh. Goulash is pretty much a mixture of any food you throw into a pot together, kind of like stew. You're okay, eat up, no boots." He chuckled again.

I looked a little doubtfully at his stocking feet as I raised my spoon the rest of the way to my mouth. Well, it didn't gag me. It was alright but the images of chopped up and boiled boots were too much to erase altogether. I was still determined to eat what could only be identified in its natural environment with the naked eye from now on. Cosmopolitan, my foot!

Me Scared? Of Cows?

The Big Stream as we so named it, or more accurately as Leo and Andy so named it, was due north of us about three miles by the estimation of an honest crow's flight. It meandered through farm and field, woodland and aspen groves. It afforded us youngsters countless hours of adventuring with our slingshots, bow and arrows, or just exploring.

A while back, I walked back to this Big Stream as we children had done so many times through our childhood. I stood on the spot where a beaver pond once stood, all traces of its dam since vanished with time; but the same stream, the same aspen trees, the same frogs a singing their spring serenades greeted me. The late evening, early spring sun warmed my back as my gaze melded with my memory. A very leaning aspen tree shimmered together with that same leaning aspen tree that I had so many times climbed, as I watched a young magpie grow in its nest.

You might remember that that's the very one a raccoon got to first and the little magpie became his lunch instead of my pet. Now, having enjoyed the balm of this blend of current natural delight and nostalgic sensations, I wandered upstream so as to capture more of these happy reminisces. When to my immense surprise and delight, I espied a huge bull moose feeding halfway across the crick and standing amongst the aspens. It had spotted me, too, and we gazed intently at each other. I had never seen a moose with a grey coarse-haired cape. He looked gigantic, old, majestic and a bit scary. Adult bull moose can be very cantankerous; so I looked around to see where the nearest tree I could climb was, in case he decided I had breached the bounds of social graces and he chose to chase me from his domain. I began to laugh inside myself as there I stood face-to-face with a bull, just like I had so many years before. Only the bull I faced in my childhood was not a moose, but the herd bull owned by the farmer whose land I trod.

Back then, I was about 11ish. I was crouched down in the densest part of a thicket I could find in my haste, water slowly soaking through the seams of my shoes, hands clutching my bow and arrow as I lay hopefully concealed from a very angry, bellowing, approaching bull.

Now I don't know where I had developed my fear of other people's cows. We had cows during my entire life, and I liked them. I never got seriously hurt, although near escapes and some bruises and abrasions acquired in the herding and caring for them sometimes decorated my limbs. But other people's cows are different.

In almost every field we traversed in our adventuring and in most woods one would invariably run into a herd of cows. Now cows are very naturally curious beasts and even though most of these herds were quite wild, they would run towards us when spotted to find what these skinny little boys accoutered with primitive weapons were. Now a whole herd of cows coming a running is different say than a herd of mice with a case of the curios. Mice weighing in at about the same as three quarters and a dime all in a heap is not that intimidating, but when cows come hauling in weighing in about 12 stevedores each, that's a different story altogether. And that's why I am telling this story and not the one about the mice, however nice.

Now Jeremy was not particularly scared and neither were the other boys, but when you found us wandering through a farmer's field you could be sure my eyes were swiveling around, looking for the inevitable cows and the closest fence. And sure enough there would be the herd. Up would pop the head of one of the feeding cows. Its eyes filled with wonderment. Than as if by cue, up would pop another, and then by some kind of bovine telepathy, all would pop up and a wave would start towards us. My pace would pick up, slowly at first, then with a little more urgency. Trying to keep dignity in tow, and with Jeremy saying assuredly, "They're not going to get us." I would try to affect a nonchalance attitude while I looked over my shoulder and hurried really fast. And then the cows would start to run. And then pandemonium would break loose. Cows lose all sense of propriety when excitement overtakes them. There's just so little excitement in a cow's life. It's quite comical.

Here you have cows, basically a bag of bones with a hide draped over to hide all the machinations that go into changing grass into milk, with a huge udder swollen with the day's work swinging like a huge lantern under them, practically throwing them off their feet as the racing and cavorting, hightailing and bucking in their excitement goads them on towards us. And here's me looking equally ridiculous as I try my darndest not to run while pumping my limbs as fast as they can go just short of full panic.

Then there was the barbwire fence. You hoped for an ancient rusted three or four strand saggy barb wire fence, which was just a minor suggestion to the cows that they might want to stay on their own property. These you can shoot through with maybe a small scratch or little tear on the clothes, but nothing to write home about. But if this were a modern dairy herd as just encountered, what you got was a four or five strand, shiny gray, tight as fiddle stringed barb wire fence with the ghastliest barbs bristling from every strand. What to do? You couldn't shoot through it. You had to go through every move of climbing through as if you had all morning, only 10 times as fast. Gingerly grab a wire and press down, reach above your bent over twisted back and gently grasp the upper wire, slowly separate the two. Put one leg through. Pants now caught on top wire, move slowly back to release that barb, other leg pant now caught on bottom wire. Cows are getting closer. Look over your shoulder to see what to do. Slingshot sticking from your belt now grabs top wire as a barb stabs your head. Cows are very close now. Release bottom hand from wire to throw bow and arrow through the fence. Bottom wire now slaps the inside of your leg with a nasty barb. Hot cow breath causes all caution to be cast to the winds. Attempt to lunge through the fence. Lunge is impossible.

A gigantic struggle ensues as you attempt to extricate yourself from said fence. With great effort you sproing (yes Webster would prefer sprang but he wasn't there, I definitely sproing) from the taut wires to the ground on the safe side of the fence. Blood flows from a number of leaks caused by your war with the barbs. You can expect no mercy from barbarians. Tattered clothes and gashes tell their story. Pick up your bow and arrow with what little nonchalance might be hanging about, as you make it through the fence. You then muster up the nastiest look possible on your face from which to cast a withering glare at those maniacal bovine matrons—from the safe side of the fence, of course. They aren't even looking. They are all eating as placidly as any lazy herd on a summer day. What! These killer cows all nice now. After watching me disgorged from the claws of the barbarian fence they had lost all interest.

Surprise a herd of beef cattle in a thick woods, added a different dimension. Sneaking along like an Indian Brave and quiet as a moccasined mouse on a malleable mattress would I be, when suddenly one of the steers masked in the thicket would sense my presence and flee uncontrolled into the brush. The crashing and smashing of tree limbs and brush raised such a noise that the entire herd took off in flight. But in what direction did they flee? None of them had a clue of where the danger originated, so they just ran in whatever direction they happened to be facing. This left me crouched in terror expecting the thundering hoofs of one of the frightened steers to run me over without even knowing I was there. When the last of the fleeing animals were heard in the distance all hope of seeing game vanished with them. I just forgot to mimic moccasined mice and trudged along like a flustered lead booted louse. There wouldn't be game within a hundred miles of that thundering noise.

And that's what leads this time to me and the bull. Jeremy and I were hunting ruffed grouse with our bow and arrows. Jeremy snuck along the north shore of the Big Stream and I snuck along the left shore.

We threaded our way amongst the aspen trees, and crouched through tunnels the cows had made through the thick brush. Away off in the distance I heard the lowing of cattle. No problem, I thought the cows were a long way off. I snuck farther in, trying to surprise a grouse. The cattle lowing again caught my attention and this time it seemed a bit closer. Hmmm? I continued to hunt. Suddenly I was aware that the cattle mooing were very much closer. They were definitely moving in our direction. Then I began to hear their hoofs as they pounded the ground, and I could definitely tell they were stampeding straight downstream where we were concealed in the brush. I was down in the marsh where the cows had pogged the ground with their hooves as they moved through the aspen grove.

Stepping gingerly on little mounds of grass that stuck up from the water, I tried not to slip off and into the water. Hearing the cows coming, I could tell they were going to parallel me up on the dry ground to my right. I didn't want to remain in one of the tunnels of bushes. What if a cow came blundering through the tunnel and finds me blocking it? I didn't relish the thought of being pogged myself into the marsh grass, so hurriedly I leapt from clump to clump heading for dryer ground out of the brush; but still not wanting to be spotted by those cows.

The entire herd was now thundering nearer and I wanted to get to a place I could hide, but not get run over. I drew up to a dense thicket right next to black pine trees, out of the tunnels but where I could crouch and peer through the brush at the passing cows. They wove their way through the small pines, snapping and popping the dried limbs as they crashed themselves through the trees. I have no idea what spooked them, but they ran crazily along in their stampede to get away. I crouched in fear as they thundered by. Finally my white knuckled hands that clutched my bow relaxed a little as the last fleeing steer disappeared in front of me. I had survived.

Arrahhh! I had just stood up when a loud bull bellow crashed through the air right behind me. Unbeknownst to me the head bull was trailing the herd. He was mad. He was really mad! His bellow originated in his huge chest and rushed like a hurricane of wind and sound from his throat, as he lifted his head to let out his angry protest. It seemed to nearly tear my head off as he walked straight toward my thicket. Could he see me in here?! How could he? What did I do? Why did he need those massive horns for any way? Brandishing them around as if he owned the place! Oh wait, he did. How'd in the world did he sneak up so close when I thought the whole herd had gone by? I looked around for the nearest tree to climb. That was wasted effort. They seemed to lean back if anything. They weren't about to be thrashed with the horns of this angry bull for harboring a hunted hunter. I had to stay put. I seriously considered sending out a distress call to Jeremy. But wait, if I did that the bull would know for sure that I was in there. Besides, what was Jeremy to do? Play matador to a 2,500-pound bull? Although the spectacle seemed like an interesting one and would afford a distraction for me to scurry up a reluctant tree, I wasn't sure yet that the bull was after me. He might just pass by.

It's a lot easier to see out of a thicket than it is to see into one and he just might not see me. His huge frame swayed as he advanced in anger towards where I was hiding, bellowing and hollering and at times stopping to paw the ground, throwing huge clods of dried ground in a cloud of dust up over his shoulder. I squatted half in fear and half in awe. I had never seen such a display of power before. Now if he continued in this way it was going to be me or him. It would be me playing matador. My little wooden arrow seemed a pretty paltry sword against this big bull, and my pocket knife seemed a downright pitiful dagger. My red handkerchief would have to do for the cape. Surely the roar in my ears was the sound of the crowd shouting from ringside at a Spanish bullfight.

The bull stepped within feet of my hiding place and seemed to pause with a suspicious angry air and stared belligerently at my bush. I checked my arsenal of weapons at my disposal with bow and arrow shaking in my hand. Check. Pocket knife crouched, trembling in my pocket. Check. Handkerchief blanching from courageous red to cowardly white crumpled in my hand. Check. Wet shoes ready for running. Check.

He stared in silent concentration. I held perfectly still trying to stare him down in turn. And I did. He moved on. I had scared him (or he didn't see me, Jeremy's unreliable opinion)! He bellowed his outrage again as he tossed his defiant head and passed, and I realized that the roar was the blood pounding in my ears as my heart tried to pound manly courage in my quivering shaking little boy body.

It almost worked. I had nearly become a matador. What a striking figure I would have cut on the marquee, my full 78-pound figure drawn to its full 5-foot, 1-inch height looking haughtily down on the brown, horned 2,500-pound fire- breathing bull. As it were I shook a little as I crept from my hiding place, my legs a little weak. I listened intently to make sure his bellows continued to mellow in the distance.

I continued my hunt. My nerves were so distraught that every little squirrel cough made me jump and turn, expecting another beast to have sneaked up to me. When I crossed over the beaver dam and met Jeremy, I recounted my story. He had heard the commotion alright, but couldn't see what was going on due to all the trees and brush. As usual, the recounting had us into stitches of laughter as the humorous side of all things scary.

Mine and other people's curious cows just never saw eye-to-eye. I made sure we didn't.

BREAD

Just as the Bread of Life is necessary for the life of the soul, Mom provided the bread of life for the body. Yes, it was Mom's bread that built us. It was this that glued the sinews of our frame together. It was this that built the bones that muscles eventually clung to. It filled the kitchen with its inviting aroma as it baked and then filled our bellies with its delightful taste as we ate it after hot oatmeal in the morning, ate it as sandwiches for school, ate it again as a snack when we arrived home from school to fill the gap until dinner; and then ate it as dessert after dinner was enjoyed. It was that good. And it was nutritious, too. It was baking powder bread, not yeast, and so it was much heavier bread. It had staying power when consumed, a complete meal in itself. The problem was that it tasted so good that even after eating a complete meal, we still reached for Mom's bread to complete the culinary repast. It was just the finish the palette needed to be fully satisfied.

A testament to this was the time when we were little and a cousin of ours from California, who was about 18 at the time, came up to Washington to spend a few days with us. Country fare was not his usual supper, but he ate two hearty helpings of Mom's meat and potatoes that nearly burst the buttons off his shirt. It had his eyes popping out like a fish out of water, but he found even he could fit in some of Mom's bread. It wasn't easy to persuade him to try it. He was already very full, packing more in to his stomach seemed futile at best and dangerous at worst. But we enjoined, and pleaded with him to try Mom's bread as we were confident he would like it, and so he eventually caved to our pleas and Mom carved him off a thick slice and slapped it onto his plate. Butter was duly passed and so was Mom's plum jam. Not any plum jam, this was a marvel in itself. She made it from plums we picked from our fruit trees. We were a reluctant bunch in the picking of them, but it sure took no persuasion to eat it. It was delicious. It just seemed a natural marriage between Mom's jam and her bread. The result was simply sublime. Like a good marriage the two were completely compatible.

James, that's our cousin, followed the proper ritual and married the two right there on his plate. He then took as deep of a breath that he could under the circumstances and took a bite. After a few chews and a swallow a look of pure delight lit up his face. He chewed with a little more gusto and then with a will. Eagerly anticipating each new bite, he plowed through three thick slices. Well, he was able to swallow these three slabs and was eyeing a fourth when conscience from the moral realm reminded him about gluttony, and from the earthly paradise of our table, his stomach was plotting mutiny. These two allies together forced him to stop. But his eye still strayed to the loaf of temptation a time or two.

Indeed, it was good bread. Mom baked an average of four loaves a day; six was not infrequent, for a jot and a little over 20 years resulting in a grand total of nearly 27,000 loaves. It was a tidy sum by any estimation.

We tried a time or two to help her with the making of the bread. We couldn't do it. Mom had developed what we called her bread arm. She never used a mixer either mechanical or electric. No, she stirred and whipped that heavy dough by hand with a huge spoon in a massive bowl. Around and around that spoon would fly as she crooked the bowl in her left arm and pinned it to the table. Egg, milk, baking powder, flour and whatever else she threw in there was battered into thick, gooey dough. Her stirring was impossible to imitate. We boys, even as we moved through our high school years what with bucking bales for the farmers, digging fence post holes or any other of the farm chores that hardened our muscles, were no match for Mom's bread arm. After Mom had thrown the ingredients in the bowl, our chivalrous spirit would prompt us to offer,

"Here, let me mix that."

"Okay that would be nice." She would say as she handed us the big spoon.

This was going to be easy. What's a couple, 3 pounds of flour in comparison to a 100-pound bale? We'd try to mimic Mom by cradling the bowl in our left arm and pinning it to table, than clench the spoon and start twirling. At first the going was easy. As the separate ingredients began to mix together it became harder, and then in direct proportion to the more it mixed, the more difficult it became until it was near impossible to turn the congealed mass at all. With our arm nearly exhausted and sweat beginning to pop forth, draining down our foreheads and threatening to spoil the dough, we would try to keep the spoon churning. With a mighty push we would lean into the spoon only to have it unceremoniously unlatch from the sticky dough and leap out of the bowl, throwing what flour was still loose around the room and spattering dough about our persons and any other unfortunate onlooker. Exhausted, we dejectedly gave the spoon to Mom to salvage what she could from our noble but failed help. She tucked that bowl and commandeered that spoon and away she'd go as if that batter were soft butter. Around and around and there it would be done. We could only marvel. Technique and a toned muscle could not be bested. Nobody could do what she could. So the task remained hers.

I was in about second grade when Tristan was born and this thrust Dad into the dual role as breadwinner and bread maker as Mom was laid up in the hospital. He could make the bread tolerably well. If you disregarded the few uncooked flat pieces that hadn't risen on account of the baking powder not being thoroughly mixed, or the clumps of dry flour interspersed around the loaf, you could get along tolerably well also. What made it particularly exciting for us kids, though, was what Dad did to the bread on purpose.

One such thing was when he put food coloring in the batter. To this day I don't know how he did it, but when he baked the bread and then sliced the loaf, the slice would have concentric rings of color starting from the outside by the crust and working in. There were different colors, too. Green on the outside and then red and yellow as it approached the center. It looked really neat to us, but it caused real consternation to our classmates at lunchtime when we opened our sandwich bags and unwrapped what looked like bread in various stages of sickness and decay. "What is that?" They would point and recoil, horrified. "Are you going to eat *that?*" Again aghast. We would just smile smugly, open our eyes wide and take a huge bite, relishing the bread and the discomfiture of our classmates at the same time. It didn't quite rise to the level of eating insect innards or snails as they do in foreign countries, but it did raise us to celebrity status for a few glorious moments.

The next day Dad introduced another innovation. He baked the bread in a large rectangular cake pan. So now when one cut off a slice with the knife, it was a long skinny piece of bread. It made eating it more like how a snake eats, starting from head to tail. It appealed to the imaginations of us little boys. Dad's monkeying around with the bread in these ways kept us from missing Mom's absence as much as we would have without these distractions. That, and just to see Dad in the kitchen doing cooking duties, he being such a masculine, powerful man, was such an anomaly in itself; it provided us with much laughter and entertainment to see him is this unnatural mode. A time or two he would even don Mom's apron. It sure looked silly and we about split our guts laughing. After having teased as much diversion as he could from these incongruities in the kitchen, he happily relinquished these domestic duties to Louisa and Elizabeth.

Mom's bread became quite popular at school after some of our friends had tasted it. They thought it looked more like cake than bread and were curious as to how it tasted. They really liked it and we could use it as a trade item. One half sandwich for two cupcakes and so on. Mom discouraged us from this practice as what we wanted to trade for had little nutritional value and we were robust youngsters needing all the calories that could be pumped in. So we mostly held onto our bread.

There was a few times, though, when we were glad

to let go of it. This would happen when Mom would forget to put the baking powder in.

"Oh dear! Oh my goodness!" We would hear Mom in a very disconsolate voice saying. "I must have forgotten to put the baking powder in." We would jump up and run into the kitchen to see what was up. Sure enough, there would be Mom bent over the oven looking down on flat hard loaves of bread. "All that work for nothing. All the work to do it over again," were the words clearly written on her crestfallen face. There wasn't much to do, but with a sigh lift them onto the hot rack to let them cool, so that she did. We weren't much help. We just didn't have the bread arm.

One day Peter knocked these loaves of bread from the bread pans and threw the pads of flattened hard pan into the pasture for the birds. But lo and behold the sheep saw these flying saucers of wheat bread and ran to investigate. To Peters' astonishment, the sheep took a bite, their eyes widened with pleasure and then they lit into the loaves with gusto. Thus a feeding frenzy of a flock of sheep took place, each shoving the other to see who'd get the most.

Even when the bread turned out wrong, it was still good enough to bring pleasure to some of God's creatures. Truly Mom's bread was the bread of life in its own way.

Bloated Cow

Spring brought so much beauty, what with all the new life bursting forth, but it brought a few challenges, too. One was to get the cows out to the newly green pastures without them getting sick. The problem arose because the feed they ate all winter was hay that was cured and put in barns for storage. Now you see cows are ruminants (no, that does not mean they like to think quietly a lot). When you say a cow is ruminating they take that very personally, viscerally really, in the gut. And they have four of them. Yep, that's four stomachs. And because they process their food in a peculiar way with all these stomachs things can get all mixed up and go wrong. Now within these environs there is a whole lot of flora and fauna that do a whole lot of digestion for free, all they ask is that the cow consume a goodly amount of food throughout the day and they will be happy. Only problem is that when the cow eats a different mixture of feed, as in going from dry hay to green pasture, these little helpers in the stomach get all mixed up. Some just up and die as they can't take the change in diet and others just can't work properly. This results in a very sour stomach in the cow, so much so that they can even up and give up the ghost if it gets too bad. This is because when the digestion goes all wrong it produces a tremendous amount of gas which blows the cow up like a balloon. Balloon bovines in Macy's parade might make a pretty sight way up in the air, but a farmer wants no such antics in his cows. It is far too dangerous. If the cow insist on blowing herself up too far she can die.

Now if the unhappy situation arises, when the cow has eaten too much fresh green pasture grass after her long winter, ends up with bloat, one must try to get this gas out of her. This is by means of bovine burps. She must be made to burp. Not a most pleasant topic in itself, but the tale I will tell lends itself to some humor.

Most of you I am sure were able to elicit a beautiful picture in your mind when I said the cow must be burped. A homey scene of a farmer with his sick cow in his lap, the cow's head flung over the farmer's shoulder and he patting the cow vigorously on the back, swam in your imagination. Just as by the same means your good mother had done to get you comfortable after your having supped on a repast of milk. Now, the good husbands who lose their fair share of sleep strolling youngsters back and forth across the floor trying to get an infant to burp, draws the line at animal husbandry using quite the same methods. It makes him downright grumpy. Sixteen hundred pounds of beef draped over one's shoulder makes for a very cozy condition, indeed, but after burping a few in this wise one just gets plumb worn out. No, the farmer must look for more vigorous and timely means.

We got a chance to watch some of these means practiced on our cow June one early spring day when she got the bloat. I was really little at the time, 4 or 5 and wasn't much use for setting things straight, although my young pride was a bit wounded when I wasn't even asked. The older kids were at school and Dad was at work, and before Mom had noticed or was told that something was wrong with the cow, her situation had advanced into a far state and needed quick remedial action. It was a perfect situation for superman or me. But no, Mom threw us all into the 1955 station wagon and headed for Mrs. Wiggins' place. She was a farmer's wife who knew a few things about farming. She would surely know what to do. A quick word with her and we were back at the house. She told us to try to get June to stand up and walk. Sometimes walking would be enough to squish things around a bit and get her into a bovine belch, again unpleasant, as it's not quite the same as new baby's or puppy breath; no this belch could wither a stiff spine at 40 or so feet but it had to be done. Jeremy, me and Jake strove manfully to rock her onto her feet, but she would have none of it.

Minutes later, to our surprise and delight, Mrs. Wiggins came cantering down the driveway on her horse. She carried a satchel of goods that she would use in her ministrations on June.

Now Mrs. Wiggins was a character herself. A tall lanky cowboy on a horse she was not. No, short and stocky was her stature, we kids questioningly checking to be sure if horse and rider hadn't better to have been switched. Her stature, her reddish hair, her non-stop talking and can-do confidence told us that we were in capable hands. The first thing she did after dismounting was to practically lift that cow onto her feet, but even with her prodigious weight the cow was a bit much and refused to stand.

So she plied her remedies in this order. Gentle at first and then if it didn't work more severe measures. First, she extracted a pop bottle from the bag's innards and next a box of baking soda bicarbonate. She asked for some water, and when receiving this she mixed up the water and baking soda in the bottle. This she tried to insert into June's mouth. Now you must remember that June had a dangerous set of horns and even though Mrs. Wiggins was fitted with an extra layer of fat it was still dangerous to have June swinging her head about trying to avoid the bottle. Mrs. Wiggins grabbed a hold of June's horn with one hand and with the other hand tried to push the bottle into June's mouth. But June clenched her teeth and thrashed about and Mrs. Wiggins, now breathing a bit harder, gave that up. Not gave up, we could see she would never *give* up. She filled the bottle once more.

She got up from the ground and asked us boys to find her a stick about yea big. Since you can't see her fingers, yea meant about 1 foot long and 2 inches thick. We ran for the woods and found a stick. She in the meanwhile cut a length of rope about 2 feet long that she had in her satchel. This she tied to one end of the stick when we handed it to her and knelt down by June's head, placing the stick and rope in her lap. She now grabbed June's mouth with both hands; one on one side and the other pushed her thumbs into the side of her mouth against the gums. June tossed her head to resist, but in so doing opened her mouth wide. Mrs. Wiggins, still holding onto June's mouth with her left hand, released her right and grabbed the stick from her lap and slapped it sideways in June's mouth. Quick as a wink she swung the rope around the back of June's head and around the free end of the stick as June's powerful tongue tried to push it from her mouth. Mrs. Wiggins had been too quick for June and now June's mouth was propped open. Mrs. Wiggins dumped the bottle into her mouth, but what do you know, June refused to swallow. Things were getting a little urgent now. June's breath was laboring and a cow can suffocate if things get too far.

The ever resourceful Mrs. Wiggins reached once more into her bag and pulled out a rubber hose about

2 feet long. This she inserted into June's mouth and threaded it down her throat. When she could see she had reached beyond the reflexes of the throat she had June licked. Up she picked that bottle of soda water and began to pour it down the tube. June could see now that she was no match for the wily Mrs. Wiggins and let her put a few bottles of her elixir down. Still, none of that pressurized air was in a hurry to get out and things were reaching a point of no return. Things had to get moving fast and Mrs. Wiggins moved to the next step.

All that soda water is called a basic in chemistry and when it meets with an acid they sort of cancel each other out. This could help stop the overly acidic stomach from producing so much gas. Mrs. Wiggins had to get this all mixed up in June's stomach and also try to get June to burp some of it out. Moving and mixing is what she needed so she called in the horse for help. She looped her lariat around June's horns and ran it to the saddle horn of the horse. She mounted and began very slowly to pull on June. Now June was laying on her side in agony and had no wish to stand up. At first she put up with the mild discomfort, but as her neck began to stretch she struggled a bit. Then in the realization that the determined Mrs. Wiggins was going to make her get up or make her into a giraffe, she made a painful but valiant effort to get up. Mrs. Wiggins let up on the rope a bit to let June gather her strength and then began to pull again. This time June heaved herself to her feet. This was an excellent turn of affairs. If we were not able to get her up it would have virtually been too late to do anything. But as it were here she was standing.

In the cow's mind she'd done enough. But not in Mrs. Wiggins' mind. Mrs. Wiggins wanted movement, action and a lot of it, to get things moving. She once again began to pull, her horse having to dig its hooves in hard and muscle down to pull with a will as June had planted her feet and was resolute not to walk. Her attitude stayed thus until the vertebrae in her neck began to complain loudly. They told June that either she begins to walk or they would no longer hang together. No, they would all go their separate ways leaving lots of space between them. June had just a moment to ruminate on this in her mind, her gut having stopped ruminating and causing all the problem. In this short rume, the long rumination not possible, and as her neck stretch was becoming a problem, she could see her neck elongated enough to look *over* the moon, which might work out in fairy tales, as no one said it did any harm to the cow who *jumped* over the moon but she had no wish to be any more immortalized in fairy tales as she was already working pretty hard to be immortalized in this one. So she began to walk. Not a comfortable walk. She looked like a wine barrel on four stiff legs, she was blown so taut. Mrs. Wiggins was not satisfied that this much activity was having the desired affect and insisted that June run.

Well, the horse did get going enough to make June run. It was quite a sight as we watched our rotund Mrs. Wiggins riding cowboy and our cow running and tossing its head in pain and indignation, practically being dragged on the end of the lariat by its horns across the pasture. But it worked. All that pent up air had decided it had enough being confined in such a tight place and sought the nearest route out. June belched and bellowed as Mrs. Wiggins dragged her unwilling and complaining patient back and forth across that pasture until she was satisfied that the job was done. This was decidedly past the time that June thought the job was done and when released from the rope and had her mouth untied, she bawled in protest and ran off to her calves.

Well, Mrs. Wiggins saved our family cow that day and provided us little boys with lively sport. We learned a valuable lesson about how to slowly introduce cows to new spring pastures and in the future when we suspected of any beginning to bloat we prodded them with sticks and made them run until they had burped themselves to health.

TV Trash

This tale must be told by the use of Leo's memory and my pen. I was not long into this wonderful world at the time and suckling and simpering were about all the trouble I could muster. It's about the day the TV died.

The TV has become a fixed piece of furniture in the American household. It had fought off books, pianos, fiddles and conversation that once filled homes with harmonious cadences, soothing and elevating to the soul. It had a brief skirmish with radio. In a few short years it knocked it off its perch and stood as the unconquerable idol of the American home. This idol advertised a TV dinner, which it promised to feed those who would give it its undivided attention. You see, it had to defeat the one rival that remained: the kitchen table and the dinner thereon. It had to wrest the table from the grip of those families who insisted on eating around it. The TV brooked no rivals and so it designed this food, which starved the table of its necessity and brought the family into the living room where it could eat, uninterrupted by music, conversation, play, or any other pesky distraction.

Who could argue with the pleasure of being able to eat salted cardboard dinners while absorbing programs that allowed you to enjoy all the adventures of the world without ever having to lift a finger or expend any precious energy? Energy so important to reserve for making money with which to buy all those things the TV said you must have to keep up with your neighbor. You didn't have to actually use them. There were storage units designed to swallow those up, so you had time to make more money and watch more TV. What a life! What endless possibilities!

So Americans set up a proper throne on which perched this new idol and gave it all the attention it deserved. One could be plumb worn out what with all this TV adventuring, so you must retire to your bedroom to get some much-needed sleep. Lo and behold you discover that the idol had spawned a child and there on the bedroom dresser where once Grandpa's and Grandma's picture reposed was a baby idol. Conversation with your spouse was virtually irrelevant and really not possible with all the important last minute messages the wisdom TV had to impart, not least of which the Late Night Show on how to get a good night's sleep by notable family Dr. Sleep. The few children who managed to be born, after all, this idol demanded full-time attention, were raised by the capable hands of this new mechanical Mom until the cycle was completed and the children grew up enslaved to its allure.

A marvelous thing happened, though, house sizes grew in direct proportion as families shrank. Now houses have 32 rooms and 12 bathrooms, with 1.8 children in them, whereas before you were lucky to get three rooms and these with eight children in them sharing one lonely bathroom. Yes, things have improved considerably.

Now the TV death I will relate did not take place in a house with 32 rooms. No, it's quite the contrary. It took place in the minuscule living room of a tiny two bedroom house on the outskirts of town with two parents and nine children. This is where our family lived for a time before Dad was able to purchase property and populate it with the next six children.

TV had only shortly before begun muscling its way into the American home. But it was advancing with considerable alacrity and few could resist the overwhelming wave. TV fever had hit and everyone was catching it. That is everyone, but not our Dad. Tools are tools and some have very limited use. And Dad could see that this one could have a very deleterious effect on the family if allowed out of it very limited confines. So he resisted this wave and never bought a TV. This was seen by friends and neighbors as simply a way of him saying that he couldn't afford one and so they plied him with payment plans, advertisements and reasons why this gregarious guest would be so good to be invited into the house.

Pressed on all sides, there came a day that a good friend of his purchased the latest and best model and insisted that Dad take his old one. After much protestation and refusing, Dad accepted as he could see that his refusals could try their friendship and the gentleman really thought he was doing him a favor.

So it entered the sacred environs of the home. At first its presence was barely felt. Soon it demanded a little more attention. Than its magnetic personality began to attract a certain loyalty until the day it held its viewers' captive.

The Lone Ranger, the cowboy hero was rounding up bad guys as Dad and the children watched with rapt attention. Dinner was done on the stove and Mom came from the kitchen door and said.

"Dinner's ready," and returned to the kitchen, but with no acknowledgment from Dad or the children.

A few minutes later Mom again rounded the corner and a little more loudly and a little impatiently said,

"Dinner's ready, everybody come and sit down." She left again. Nobody moved.

The third time she entered the room there were a few tears, as she said imploringly.

"Dad, dinner's ready". This time it registered. Dad looked away from the TV directly at her. Leo looked attentively at this exchange at the sound of Mom's voice and the tears. He saw Dad ponder silently for a moment, get up slowly from the couch, walk over to the TV, reach down and pull the plug. The Lone Ranger was stopped dead in his tracks. Not a good thing to stop a good guy in the middle of his work, but the plug was pulled on the bad guys, too, so they couldn't do any more harm either.

All the kids stared in silence as Dad moved. After having pulled the plug, he wrapped the cord around the TV. He picked it up and carried it to the back door where balancing it on one knee, he reached for the door handle and opened the door. All eyes turned and watched. The door stayed wide open. Dad could be seen walking to the garbage can. Once again he balanced the TV on his knee, reached down and took the lid off, letting it fall to the ground. With slow, gentle and measured movement, he lowered the TV into the garbage can. With a ritualistic grave movement, he reached down and picked the lid from the ground and placed it solemnly, but firmly, on the can top. The TV was duly buried.

The beast had been slain. The idol was toppled from its throne. A choice had been made. Judgment and character had won. Written in Mom's face and displayed on the table was what would be lost if the TV were allowed to stay. Dad had realized at that moment that the threat to a wholesome family life was so great, as evidenced by his partial slavery and the slavery of his children were already displaying, that it must be removed and not have a chance to wreak its havoc.

From that day on we never had a TV. All the living, loving, laughing and adventuring was done under the loving gaze of a different God, the one that Dad and Mom and we kids bent our heads over our dinner to that evening with thanksgiving. And it was the one who ruled our home from thence forth.

The Troll

"Stop pig! Stop pig!" I screamed. "Stop pig! Stop pig!"
I screamed again, trying frantically to distract a pig
from eating my troll. It wasn't so much that I had a
soft spot for trolls in general. I had applauded enthusiastically when the third Billy goat gruff had butted
the mean troll off the bridge in Grimm's fairy tale. But
this was my troll. I had chanced upon it on the playground in second grade and eagerly snatched it up.
It had been discarded there and lay forlornly looking
up for some little kid to bring it home. It was a tiny

troll not more than 1-inch tall and I couldn't find the owner.

You see, these were the troll days. A troll fad had swept the country and every little boy and girl just had to have one. To be troll less was almost unbearable. Most troll dolls were about 4 inches tall, but they came in all sizes. They looked all the same, only varied in size and color. Most were tan. Mine was green. It was a tiny green troll. They were so ugly that they were kind of cute.

Now one of the requirements of being a troll in good standing was that it had to sport an extraordinary amount of hair. Sadly, my troll was hairless. The bodies of the troll dolls were bare but the heads were not. Something had to done, and when one has eight older siblings, likely one could be pressed into service to remedy almost any situation. It was Louisa who took pity on my plight. She took yarn and painstakingly constructed a whole head full of hair for my troll. A little tiny green troll with an immense amount of blue yarn for his hair, and I loved it. I carried it all around, made caves in the dirt for it, put it in toy airplanes, flew it about, and put it under my pillow at night. It went where I went. And this takes me back to where we started.

One spring, sunny Saturday afternoon, Mom asked if I would take the table scraps and throw them over the fence for the pigs. This just entailed a few scraps of bread and I took them from her hands and cradled them in mine. Out the back door I went to the pig pen. The pig wire was considerably higher than I was and it took quite a toss to throw them over the fence. So I cocked my arm back and threw with all my might. Up and over sailed the bread crust. But horror, my troll sailed with the scraps also! There he was snuggled in a crust of bread as it flew a huge arc over the fence. As the bread came crashing to the ground my troll lay there in the dirt amongst the bread crust. The pig ran eagerly to it, opened its big toothy mouth and began slopping up the crusts. And pigs do slop. It's no use trying to teach them not to slop, it just makes you angry and irritates the pig. Just try teaching them to sing has the same effect. Well, I wasn't trying to teach a pig to sing. I was screaming at the peak of my ability to strike fear into it. It was to no avail. The pig slopped its way through the crust and then snuffled my troll. "Oh please let the smell and tickle of the yarn disgust it." It was not to be. It noisily slurped my troll right into its mouth, crunched a few satisfying crunches and swilled him down. All the while I was jumping up and down, screaming, "Stop pig! Stop pig!" I never got any more inventive, but just became more frantic. My screams trailed off in despair as I witnessed my troll disappear in this most undignified way.

I couldn't have done much else. Even if I could have gotten the gate open, what was I to do with this 300-pound lump of lard? Kick it? It wouldn't feel it. Kiss it? Revolting to me, however flattering it may have been to the pig. No, I just screamed. In one of those rare moments on the farm there was no one to rescue me. Neither Jeremy nor Jake were there to sail over the fence. Leo nor Andy near, and Dad was at work. The girls were gone and so the fate was sealed on my troll. I couldn't cry at first, I was so stunned at the rapidity that the whole thing happened, so I just meandered back to the house in shock. When I told Mom, I tried not to cry but I feared with all my manly effort the sorrow of my loss extracted sobs. It was a bitter pill to swallow.

But I suppose, not for long. Like so many heartbreaking times in childhood, it passed quickly and I was off to more adventures. The tragic troll story, filed away along with the memory of Louisa's kindness in troll tress making, was one of the many that formed my character along life's path.

SACRIFICE

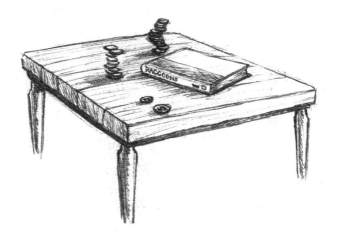

I hunkered down between the bottom bunks of two of the bunk beds and counted out the number of acorns as they each fell from the mouth of an old baby food jar. Seventeen, 18, 19, 20, what a nice round number I mused. I had collected these acorns from the park when our school had its end of the summer picnic. We didn't have acorns growing wild and so the park was the only source available. Since our farm and its surroundings were a veritable park, we never as a family used the city's park. Consequently, this was a precious find for me. You see, I was saving up food for a raccoon that I dreamt of getting. It was only a dream, but it was almost as real to me as life. I don't remember when I first fell in love with coons, but by this time I had filled my imagination with all the books I could get from the library that dealt with them. Having read Sterling North's, <u>Rascal</u> cemented me of the view that I must have a raccoon as my very own.

I don't think Mom or Dad were privy to my desire to actually possess one in all earnestness, but they enjoyed my chatter about coons as I told them of the stories I had read and my love for them.

I started collecting a cache of goods that I might need for it. I fashioned a little leather leash for my raccoon from some old leather cut from old spats, which Dad would bring home from work. These were heavy leather spats designed to protect his work boots from hot molten aluminum, which would occasionally splash from the huge crucibles that held it. I was collecting acorns as I could, had started collecting insects that I thought might make a tasty meal for it, but soon gave up on the idea when I found the bugs being uncooperative. After a few days of confinement, they up and expired in protest.

Most importantly, though, is I collected money. These were not big amounts of money. Over two years I had collected $7.50 towards the $12 I needed.

I had a taxidermy supply catalog I had ordered from a supplier found in the back of a Popular Mechanics magazine. The ads in the back advertised raccoon babies for $12 each.

Grandpa and Grandma would send us a dollar with a birthday card every year, that and the nickel and dimes found in the parking lots of grocery stores were added together. Occasionally, Dad would give me the change that jingled in his pocket, which all added up to the $7.50 cents I mentioned before. When I reached the $12, I planned on asking Dad for the raccoon.

Well, after counting the acorns, I dumped the money from another old baby food jar, stirring the coins around to see if they might have multiplied when I was away. They never seemed to. Our rabbits did, though. Dad said you couldn't really make money with rabbits. He probably was right, they just kept having babies. Curiously, it didn't seem you could make money with money, either; maybe you had to feed a special food called usury to get it to multiply, but I didn't have any so I had to be content by getting it by gift, finding it, or earning it if a visiting uncle required a favor. I put the money back into the jar and dreamed some more about my pet raccoon.

Not long after one of my excursions into my raccoon treasure box, Dad summoned us for a family meeting. The two events were unrelated as such, but became related after Dad related to us that our relations, Grandpa and Grandma, his parents, were going to drive up from Los Angeles to see us. Only problem was, there just was not quite enough money to cover all the expenses. If our family could pitch in to help, the long looked for happy occasion would be possible, but if not it would have to wait until his and our families pecuniary emoluments were much enhanced. It was a polite way of saying until we had more money.

There was a little money in the parental coffers that could be coaxed out to remedy this state of affairs but not enough; hence, the family council. It was proposed by Dad that he figure up a sliding scale of giving that would start from Louisa and descend down to the baby. It was not something that he required of us, but something that he proposed as act an of generosity; and with our consent, he would apprise us of the calculations he had done as to what each of our contributions would be to bring the total to what was needed. The consent would have to be unanimous so there would be no undue burden placed on any particular child. We all enthusiastically were in favor of this, to see Grandpa and Grandma would be a treat indeed. I not having any memory of seeing them previously and it was becoming a faint memory for the older ones.

It seemed the largest sum calculated for the older ones that I remember started at about $50 and went down from there. By the time it reached me it was considerably less. But the incredible happened. I listened with astonishment as my allotment to the purse would be $7.50. What, $7.50! How could this be? It certainly wasn't planned. Neither Dad nor Mom knew I was saving for a raccoon. They knew we all kept a money jar, but they didn't know how much we had in them. Dad would never have calculated such a sum for me if he knew that that was my full possession and how it would dash my hopes. I think he would have denied me a raccoon in any case, but he certainly wouldn't do it in that manner.

Could it be a coincidence? Wow, what a coincidence. Well no, more likely Divine Providence removed the possibility of my getting a raccoon to a more remote time, my imagination still supplying me with great pleasure in the thought of owning one. Over time, other interests prevailed and I relinquished the thought. I didn't say anything about my dreams for a raccoon when I handed over the money and I don't remember ever being particularly disappointed about giving up the $7.50. But what stuck indelibly all these years was that the amount would be so exactly the amount I had saved for my raccoon.

It was well worth it, though. Grandpa's and Grandma's visit was filled with fun and excitement. Remember the black eye Tristan got from the ball smote from the hands of grandpas' baseball bat? Or the five chin-ups he did on the old swing set? Well you should, I told you about them in volume one. If you are one of the unlucky few who don't have volume one, I suggest you get one because you are going to miss these other stories coming while your absorbed in getting caught up. Hurry, we're leaving for the next adventure.

DYNAMITE

When I was a small child there were just enough of the fading edges of the Old West to tame that dynamite could still be bought by local farmers, miners, loggers, or any who needed that force of a mighty blast to remove whatever obstacle they thought stood in the way of progress.

The mine that stood on our western border

became defunct just a few years into my childhood, but the memories of those last days were etched in by the sound and fury of the dynamite blast that rent the quiet once or twice a week as the miners sought the last of the ore they wished to extract. There was about a 50-yard wide swath of ponderosa pine forest that bordered our western property line that was mine property. It shielded us from most of the mining activity. There was nothing, though, that shielded us from those blasts.

One of the miners would come ambling down through the trees to inform us.

"We're going to blast in about half an hour," he would say. "Open all your windows and stay in the house until it's over." These were not hard messages to deliver as they would walk away with at least a cold drink of water and maybe some cookies if their timing was just right. In any case, we followed their instructions. We would throw up all the sashes and make sure everyone was in the house until, *Ka Boom!* The sound would hit our ears, the windows would rattle and shake, the pans and knick knacks would skip and dance on the shelves and we would wait wide-eyed until, sure enough, a rain of small pebbles would pitter patter all over our aluminum metal roof. The force of the blast would send some dirt and rock so high it would clear the top of the ponderosas and come raining down on us. When one such rock, the size of a baseball, hit in the front yard, Dad had a little talk with the miners. It didn't happen again.

We had a good relationship with those miners.

One of our favorite things to do was to get the truck drivers to blow their big air horn, which was mounted to the top of the cab of their truck. Any time we were up our road that bordered theirs by the county road, we would pump our arms up and down as hard as our little hands would. More often than not, he'd reach up to pull the steel cord mounted on the inside of his cab over his head and let loose a great blast of air through the air horn. Sometimes we would be headed into town 10 miles away from the mine on the highway and see a big mine truck coming our way. We would all start pumping our arms, all us kids packed into the big car. Sure enough, the truck driver would see our family car coming and he would reach up and let forth a huge bellow on that horn as he zoomed on by.

Well, as I was saying, before these miners started carrying my story away is that dynamite was pretty common in those days. I even met a logger years later when working as a logger in Alaska, who was missing his three middle fingers. He had lost them when he had set a charge of dynamite under a huge log he had to blast a hole in to get a steel cable under.

Well, this time it was Dad's turn, though he kept his fingers. Before Dad had the house built on our property, and before I was old enough to be any help, he took the five oldest ones, Louisa, Elizabeth, Leo, Marisa and Andy out to the property to remove a large rock from the field. Rocks in farmer's fields are often like icebergs, a little part sticks up above the soil while the ground harbors the rest of its huge bulk beneath its surface. It was like this with this rock. The plow had hit it and it hadn't moved. Only this rock looked about the size of a football. So Dad got his shovel and started to dig. Ought to be able to dig some dirt from around this and pry it loose and be on his way. The rock had other ideas. It had been perfectly happy to rest there since Noah's flood. Besides the impertinent shoves of the frost leaving the ground in spring, it had been pretty much left alone. So it hunkered down now and wouldn't budge. Dad dug some more. Hmmm. This rock was not going to be easy. Small rocks in the field are bad enough as they batter up farm implements; but big ones do serious damage, bending and breaking even the most hardened steel. The more Dad dug the bigger the rock grew, until pretty soon the football size rock became a small boulder. If it grew any bigger, even Dad would have a hard time wresting it from its entrenched position. Well, he did keep digging until it seemed that he'd hit a fossilized humpback whale. By this time Dad realized that sterner measures were going to be required. He'd turned the tractor off as it was just sitting smoking its pipe; it wasn't doing any good, but now he looked at it now with renewed interest.

First a respite with the lunch Mom had sent along and a chat with the children on the running board of the 1936 Chevy flatbed. Thus refreshed, he turned to his task again. Three feet down in the ground he finally unearthed the underbelly of the boulder beast and bored a hole under it. Around the other side he did the same. This stone did not take kindly to be tickled so under its belly and grasped more firmly to the soil where Dad hadn't dug. Next, Dad got a chain and looped it around the rock and pulled the loose end out a ways. He unhooked the plow from the tractor. The tractor looked skeptically at all this and seemed to say as it sputtered and coughed and refused to start. "You expect me to pull that out. Not me." When Dad showed it the can of nasty smelling starter fluid he threatened to squirt into the tractor's carburetor if it refused to start, the tractor hurrumppphed in one more protest and roared to life. After hooking the chain to the hitch of the tractor, Dad climbed on. He put it into low gear and eased out the clutch. The tractor inched forward and the chain tightened as it brought up the slack and started pulling on the rock. The tractor motor bogged down ready to quit, the governor on the motor cried out for more fuel and the spring on the carburetor sprung to action and poured on the fuel. The engine roared. The rock quivered under the strain, but refused to give ground. The tires gripped on the soil with all the tenacity that they could marshal, but it was not enough. They started to slip, and then to spin and the rock stayed put. It was clear the rock was too big and heavy to be pulled from its post-diluvian nest.

It was time for dynamite. Dad drove the handful of kids he had with him to the hardware store. Leo was privileged to go into the store and they went to the counter.

"I've got a rock in my field that I need to break into a few pieces, so I can get my tractor to pull them out. I can't do as it is." Dad explained to the clerk.

"What size tractor you pulling with?" The man asked, trying to get a feel of how big this rock was.

"It's a W9," Dad replied.

"My that's got to be quite a stone. Couple of sticks of dynamite ought to persuade it. There're back there." He jerked his thumb toward the back of the store. Dad purchased two and a blasting cap (the trigger or fuse) and returned to the farm.

He got a bucket of water and drove the flatbed about 60 yards from the rock and parked. He then told the kids to stay behind it, with further instructions that if it were a really big blast dive under the truck to be sure nothing could fall on your head.

He took Leo with him out to the rock explaining. "Sometimes when you insert the blasting cap it will make the dynamite explode prematurely. I want you here in case I get hurt and you can run for help." Leo felt all puffed up with pride to be Dad's helper and he watched Dad break off half a stick of dynamite. "This ought to do it, if we don't want to blow up the whole farm." He placed the half stick in the recesses of the hole next to the rock. He mixed a slurry of dirt and water into mud and placed this over the dynamite so that more of the force of the blast would be directed at the rock and not come shooting back out of the hole. He cut a fuse length to be a two minute fuse and lit it. Dad and Leo ran to the truck and stood behind it in anticipation of the blast. What seemed a lot longer than two minutes, and when the tension of expectation was almost too much to endure, there popped a sickly little explosion that barely hopped a little earth up a couple of inches off the ground. The awaited blast turned out to be a muffled little poof! What a disappointment. Dad walked out to the rock a little disgustedly at such a wimpy excuse for an explosion. The rock hadn't even been a mite bit shaken.

Shaking his head, he herded the gang back into the truck and headed back to the hardware store.

"Half a stick didn't do a thing," he told the man behind the counter. "I'll need some more."

"Well, I've had that box for a long time; there are three or four broken sticks and some good ones, which will make 10 sticks in all." Take the box. I've got to order another anyway." So Dad left the store with 10 sticks of dynamite.

Arriving at the farm again and getting more water, he parked the truck and carried his arsenal to the rock. Once more Leo followed. Dad carefully placed all 10 sticks of dynamite up tight against the rock as deep in the hole as he could. He then inserted the blasting cap and cut off a three-minute fuse this time explaining to Leo that with this much firepower they wanted to be a long way away when it blew. He then placed three buckets of mud over it and lit the fuse. Dad and Leo once again ran for the truck. Nothing happened. They hunkered down behind the truck, just peeking over and watching in fear, anticipation and excitement. Still nothing happened. They waited for what seemed like an eternity and began to squirm in impatience.

Dad explained it was best to wait a long time even if you thought it was way past time, just to make sure. Well they waited there for a long time and now there was the added danger of going up to see if it were going to blow even if it were a long time after it should have blown. Well, the waiting got the best of Dad, too, so he stepped out from behind the truck and started towards the rock. There was just a slight swell in the field about halfway there that prevented him from seeing the hole and he thought to just walk up enough to see over that swell to see if he could see any smoke from the burning fuse.

Right when he got about 30 steps out, a tremendous detonation shook the earth. It was as if a giant subterranean dragon let out a ferocious roar, spewing fire and dirt hundreds of feet into the air from its angry mouth. Dad whirled in an instant and streaked for the truck as the ground shook and trembled under his feet. His legs churned and his arms pumped, concerted effort and fear etched his drawn face as he raced. The kids, shocked momentarily into inaction, watched mesmerized, as if in slow motion. Here was Dad running, a huge umbrella of earth rising to the sky behind him, a terrific noise, and the earth quaking all around. Dad began yelling. "Under the truck, under the truck." Like squirrels popping into their holes when the shadow of hawk appears, the kids dove under the truck. From there they saw Dad fling himself to the ground and roll under with them. The earth that had been flung skyward began to rain down upon them. Pelting the truck like a hailstorm, it rained down. The roar of the blast echoed and re-echoed from the hills, rumbling into the distance as the earth tried to shake the last tremors from its mantle. Then silence, who would have thought that silence could be so quiet? Everyone was still. Dad at last broke the stillness. He said a little quietly and then joked. "Well, I guess that's one way of making gravel." He crawled out from under the truck. That loosened the tongues of all the children. They all began to exclaim excitedly about what they saw and heard and felt. With a cacophonous chatter they danced around Dad as he listened to each one of them. His nerves began to unwind as the realization that all were safe sunk in. "TEN STICKS OF DYNAMITE!"

It wasn't but a few minutes later that neighbors began appearing. First Mrs. Wiggins appeared in her old pickup. Out she bounced and said "Couldn't help but hear a bit of a boom. Is everything all right?" Dad assured her that all was well, and when she heard the story, all her rolls of fat joined in with her and rolled around laughing. "TEN STICKS OF DYNAMITE!" She coughed out trying to catch her breath.

She wasn't the last. There came Mr. O and than Mr. W and Mr. K and then pretty much the whole alphabet of neighbors came to make out what had happened. "TEN STICKS OF DYNAMITE! was said so often it almost became a battle cry. About all Dad could say was. "It works real well for getting rocks out." Sometimes a whole explanation just doesn't make sense to launch into at the time. But Dad did tell the kids later that had not he experienced the first dynamite stick being so wimpy and the fact that the agent said that what he was selling were old, he wouldn't have used so many.

The neighbors all meant well, though. Surely that blast was heard a long way away in order to bring all these neighbors in. Our nearest neighbor is a quarter of a mile away and the other farms are speckled about the prairie farther than that.

As for the rock, only a few remnants could be found skulking about. They seemed insulted for being so mistreated. The big chunks were taken to a rock pile where they still sit dejectedly pondering the glory days when they hung together and broke plowshares.

As for dynamite...that was the last Dad used of it. The miners used it for a few more years. Now only a few experts are allowed to use it, unlike in its heyday, on which we caught the tail end.

VULTURES

One day in the early spring found Jeremy and I strolling along a little lane that meandered through the black pine forest. The lane had to meander, as it followed a stream that insisted on meandering through field and wood. If it wanted to keep up it had better meander, too. And so did I. We called this stream that the lane meandered with the Big Stream, as opposed to the Little Stream, which the Big Stream had met a little ways back across a couple of pastures. The Big Stream originated all the way back on Wild Rose Prairie whereas the Little Stream crept out of Half Moon Prairie. They had met there, merged as streams tend to do even after meeting for the first time, flowed as one now and soon plunged into a stretch of thickets of cackleberry bushes.

It was in these thickets where the Big Stream ran through that we spent many hours trying to shoot ruffed grouse or rabbit or some such. Most of those adventures came later, when we were equipped with bow and arrow. But now strolling along we were a little younger and were only armed with our ever present slingshots. We came to a little fork in the lane, one fork stayed with the stream and the other wandered away and into the black pine. We struck off away from the stream to follow this lane into the forest. It was barely discernible and wandered a little aimlessly through the trees.

It was late morning, and the sun filtered down through the needles of the pine and shimmered on the aspen leaves that sprouted from the loamy terrain. We walked quietly along when suddenly Jeremy pulled up short. With an almost imperceptible motion of his, he indicated that there was something ahead. That was all it took. I looked where he was looking, just in time to see a massive bird lifting ponderously from the ground and then flying straight away from us just feet from the ground following the lane. We could barely keep it in sight as the lane ahead wove back and forth through the trees. We ran as fast as we could to try to keep it in view as it floated through the trees. We caught glimpses of it as it came in and out of sight, sometimes seeing the sun splash it as it glided along. It was too fast for us and we lost sight of it. We pulled up to a stop, panting and trying to catch our breath, which we had lost a ways back as we tried to catch the phantom bird.

We had never seen such a huge bird and were in the highest state of excitement. It seemed to disappear as quickly as it had appeared, like a mirage that seemed to vanish in the mystical morning air. When it was no more, we looked at each other and started whispering excitedly "Was that an eagle?" I asked in bewilderment. "I don't know," Jeremy replied, "a bald eagle should have a white head and tail I think." I don't even think we'd ever seen a real eagle before, so I really didn't know what to think. At this point we couldn't even be sure of the characteristics of the bird we had seen.

Did it have a long or short tail? What was its color? We both agreed it looked black. Eagles weren't really black like this, were they? Couldn't say we saw the head. It was too far ahead of us. What was clear is that it was really, really big! And we knew that we had never seen anything like it before. It made no noise, and the forest sounds continued as before.

Still incredulous, we advanced along when a stench smote our nostrils that nearly drove the wind out of us. We stopped, puzzling. Did we hear the sound of gagging maggots? Something had died that could not be forgotten. Rotten, yes. Forgotten, no. This needed to be looked into. Holding our noses as the best we could, we continued up the lane. Now it was our eyes turn to be assaulted. As it were, it was the sight of a dead cow that brought us up short.

The offensive sight and smell was both intriguing and repelling. As the little boys that we were and are wont to do, we couldn't leave well enough alone. We found sticks to poke and prod it. But even our morbid curiosity could not overcome the necessity to breath. We threw our sticks away and ran upwind. Having wrenched ourselves from the foul scene, we hurried farther up the lane, until a pristine landscape and pure air washed us clean.

We walked a little more quickly now, hashing over the phenomena of the huge bird when we were brought up short by the sight of a monstrous bird flying straight for us. Its wings seemed to stretch from one side of the lane to the other, just missing the trees standing on either side. In the mystical surrounding it could have been a Pterosaur, which was a huge dinosaur-type of bird. Not more than 20 feet off the ground it glided straight toward us. We stood riveted. Nearly as rooted as the ancient pines around us. It grew larger, it was upon us, and then with a rush of air it sailed over our head and disappeared into the forest. It took a moment before either of us could move. Then we slowly turned and looked at each other and mouthed the same words "Did you see that?" We didn't know what a rhetorical question was yet, but we felt free to use one. Who could not have seen it? It was a mythical flying beast for a mystical beautiful morning.

Once again we marveled and wondered what on earth these birds were? It was both scary and exciting. Was that the same bird or was there two? Or more? Dare we walk farther? We didn't have time to ponder because with a whoosh and re-whoosh, the sound of huge wings plying the air startled us from our baffled state. We looked around to see two or three more flying over the tree tops, bigger that anything we had seen, and the more we stood there, necks craned up into the blue sky, we counted 11 more as they flew over. When that seemed to be all of them, we ran towards where they were headed to see if we could see where they were going. We were rewarded for our efforts, because there to our immense delight and shock were the mighty birds. Perched high atop a few upper branches of a gigantic dead tree, 11 of these big birds were roosted. It was a nearly branchless spire that reached high above the surrounding forest, a snag as we called them. Only a few rotten limbs high near the top still clung to its trunk. It was on these perilous perches that sat the whole flock.

We stayed perfectly still, when snap! One of the rotten branches snapped under the weight of one of them. It struggled to hold on to a small stob with one foot. It flapped it huge ungainly wings, trying to regain its balance as its one free foot flailed around; its talons groping around for footing. This aerobatic bird show held us mesmerized. Finally, with great effort, it hooked a talon on its free claw on the small stob also and clung there. In a foul humor, with just adequate support, the great bird settled onto its perch. And with the rest of them it sat, and at them all we stared. We soaked in this sight as they soaked in the sun, until as on cue they lifted their giant wings, thrust themselves from their roost, and launched themselves into the sky and circled higher, riding on the late morning updrafts of warm air currents. Soon they were carried away far from our sight and left us.

We mulled over what we had just witnessed, trying to figure out what these big birds were. They seemed a bird with a miffed and sullen personality. They seemed kind of high-shouldered critters with a craven look about them as if they were half guilty of something.

And did they have a reddish, bald looking head? Well, they hadn't stayed long. Not so we could really get to know them. So we had a lot of unanswered questions.

So we hurried ourselves to the nearest expert on things great and small, to home and to our oldest brother Leo. He helped us put together the parts of the puzzle and what we came up with is that we had seen some buzzards. Seeing that we had startled the first buzzard from his anticipated delight of a meal of a dead cow indicated carrion was what drew these sullen folks. He likely was just ready to call his friends to dinner, after having eaten the best parts, when he was interrupted from this all natural smorgasbord by our unwanted and untimely interruption. It seemed very probable.

Now with the experiences of years we know they were California turkey vultures. That was the only time we ever saw them in our childhood.

Fifty years later there seems to be quite a few around the Pacific Northwest, but at that time I don't think their range extended that far north. The only thing I could think is that the stink of the dead cow had caught the jet stream south to Southern California and it started the migration of the California turkey vultures north. Sounds feasible, don't you think?

A Fond Farewell

I won't be catching the jet stream south, but I must corral my little children into the car and be off southeast for home. Grandma must be left alone again. A good thing for a little while maybe, but Alone can become quite a pest and will once more need to be chased away. Don't miss the next time I come to do just that. Listen for the cattle call and we'll be off to more adventuring.